The Slope

The Slope

By Janet Stevenson

Privately Printed
for the Walk of the Heroines
Portland, Oregon
2009

The Slope © 2009 Janet Stevenson

All rights reserved. No portion of this book may be reproduced—mechanically, electronically or by any means including photocopying—without written permission from the author.

ISBN13: 978-0-615-27700-4

Designed by Abbey Gaterud.
Set in ITC Legacy Sans Std and Adobe Jenson Pro.

Printed in the United States by BookMobile.

The Slope is based on episodes in the life of Dr. Bethenia Owens-Adair,
the first woman medical doctor in Oregon.
Dr. Owens-Adair is honored in the
Walk of the Heroines at Portland State University.

1.

She dismounted, pulled Pride's reins over his head, left him to forage in the sparse dune grass, found herself a hollow out of the wind and fixed her eyes on the dirty white ruffle that marked the surf line.

The tide was a run out. Sand flats, the color of wet cement, stretched into haze. The sky was lead, striped with silver where the cloud cover thinned. Gulls scavenged along the water's edge. Far to the south, a line of clam diggers moved in silhouette against the grayness, like a parade of blind cripples tapping their way among the shallows and exposed bars. Still farther south, the blue-black hulk of Tillamook Head loomed like a breaching whale.

It had looked the same forty years ago when she and her brothers came to comb the flotsam along the high-tide line. And later when she and Will were courting and came to race their horses out to the surf. Still later when she taught her son and Sister's how to find the sand dimples that betrayed a buried razor clam. Even when James brought her here the first year after they were married. The tide was higher that day, and a cold easterly wind was blowing white hair from the crests of the incoming breakers. James talked about his railroad—how it would secure their fortunes and those of other dwellers along the coast—talked with such passionate confidence that for a while his dazzling vision blotted out the gray reality that had not changed. And never would…

Nothing would ever change. The sea and the sand and the wind-clouded sky were as timeless as sin. The perspective of eternity drained the veins of her anger.

She had no business to be angry with Millie anyway. She was the victim, not the perpetrator. The same dear, good child she had always been—hardly a child at thirty, to be sure, but just as defenseless, loving, and loyal as a spaniel, without a dog's instinct for self-preservation. Trusting and submissive. Ripe for ravishment!

Who was the ravisher? That was the question.

But it was not the only one. Why had Millie not come to her, the "dearest mother," who had loved her as her own, given her an education few women could aspire to, fit her to fly on her own wings, and received her back into the nest when Millie chose not to start a practice of her own. What could have tempted her to betray the trust that love implied? And how could she have hoped to keep such a secret? She was at least four months pregnant, maybe five. Harriet had only a moment's glimpse of the girl's naked body, but the signs were unmistakable: the changed outline of the belly—Millie was so slender that her loose clothing concealed it even now—the swelling of the breasts, the darkening of the nipples. Unmistakable, but inexplicable. How could such a thing have happened?

Millie was too shy of men to stay alone in the parlor—much less walk out with one. She had her admirers in the days when they lived in the city, and Harriet had often urged her to encourage one of them. But Millie could not—or would not—conquer her shyness. If shyness it was. (Sometimes Harriet suspected it was aversion, the result of abuse the child had suffered before her birth mother entrusted her to the doctor, asking only that no word of her death or the disposition of the child carry to the ears of the drunken boor who had tormented them.)

No, it was not possible! Millie could not be carrying a child. Her eyes must have played her a trick.

She looked again, but Millie had covered herself with her wrapper and was hurrying up the stairs. The little pile of clean underclothes she had laid out to wear after her bath lay forgotten on the chair.

That was when she should have spoken. "Millie!" And when the girl stopped and turned to face her, "Is there something you want to tell Mother?"

The girl would not have been able to resist that. She would have burst into tears, thrown herself into Harriet's arms, and sobbed out her confession, naming her betrayer! Or was it her lover? (It hardly mattered which.)

And there were still other questions. Why had she, Harriet, let the moment slip? Words had formed in her mind, but something blocked their escape, something she still felt, but could not put a name to. Well, no matter. Another moment would have to be found. Perhaps Millie would choose it herself, when she was ready. But why had she waited this long? A month or even six weeks ago, she might have hoped to escape the consequences of what was probably a single act of intercourse, but she must have given up hoping by now. Millie had trained as a physician. Innocent she might be of the ways of the world, but she knew the facts of human reproduction. She knew that a man had invaded her body and left his sperm. She knew the meaning of the menses. By now she must have missed at least three periods, and she knew that her body was already proclaiming what her silence denied. Why then had Millie let the moment slip?

Because she didn't mean to speak, not ever! She had made up her mind not to betray her betrayer. Harriet was shaken by a spasm of anger. If she had the girl within her grasp, she would shake the truth out of her.

But the spasm eased, and she reminded herself that it would do no good to force the issue. Millie must be appealed to for the sake of the family whose love had given her a good life and for the sake of the child she would condemn to life without such support. She must be persuaded that confession would open the way to a happier ending for all concerned. Even for the man. That was who must be forced. Bullied or bribed or threatened to do right. James would have to see to that. It was not the sort of thing he was good at, but he had accepted Millie as a daughter, and he would do a father's duty. She could count on him for that. What he would not—could not do—was to keep the matter from his family. He would promise, but if his mother—or more likely one of his sisters-in-law—caught even a whiff of scandal, they would badger him until he had given them yet another weapon to be used against her. Harriet's cheeks were burning as if she had already endured their insults. She took a deep breath of cold wind and blew it out again.

Well, what of it? They could hardly do worse than they had done up to now. And this time they would have to keep their displeasure to themselves, have to bite their venomous tongues, nod and smile, and attend the wedding. She would arrange it so that they had no choice.

It would be held in the Episcopal Church, with a reception in the church hall afterward. There would be engraved invitations, candles and flowers at the altar, white ribbon bows at the aisle end of every pew. Everything as it had been at her wedding to James, which the Franklins had attended with such bad grace.

She would design the gowns herself. She'd had little opportunity to exercise her talent for fashion since James brought her out to this wilderness farm, where she could have gone unwashed and unkempt as she had in her childhood, for all anyone would have noticed. Her own cream-colored brocade could be taken in to fit Millie. (It had not been seen in Astoria.) For the bridesmaids, taffeta in reversed combinations of two shades of yellow. For herself, blue—royal or French—and a toque with a curled plume, dyed to the same shade. Little Rogie would act as ring-bearer in a suit of the darker yellow.

She was beginning to enjoy the planning. James would give the bride away. One of his nieces and one of hers would be the bride's attendants. The announcement to the newspapers would mention that the newlyweds would reside with Col. and Mrs. Dr. Ferry-Franklin at their farm near the Skipanon. It was far enough from town so the progress of Millie's pregnancy could not be monitored by the gossips. News of the birth would reach them only after an appropriate interval, and as attending physician, Harriet could declare the birth premature by as many weeks as need be…

Raucous screams cut through her dreaming. Two gulls were chasing another that had something in its beak. They swooped so low that Pride was startled. His hoof stamped and started a little river of dry sand down the seaward slope of the dune.

A beetle that had been climbing the slope was carried down, struggling bravely, but to no avail. By the time the sands came to rest at the angle of repose, the insect was half-buried. Harriet watched it shake itself free, lift its antennae, move them from side to side as if seeking a direction. Then, without pausing to rest, it started up the slope. The sand was so slippery that it lost half of every inch it gained, but it continued to climb, stubbornly heading toward the place from which it had been swept.

She had been doing something like that all her life—as a young wife with a shiftless and violent husband, as a divorced woman with a child to support, the disgraced daughter of a disgraced father, as a woman doctor in a world of hostile men, and lately as a mother bereaved. Each time she had finished the long upward climb, something had sent her sliding down and all but buried her.

But at least this time she did not have to climb alone. She had James. His love had been put to the test and come through stronger than before. This time she had married a man on whom she could lean for support when she needed it.

The pursuing gulls passed above her on their way back to the sea, and a dropping splattered on the sand beside her. *(Like the rotten eggs that splattered at her feet as she climbed the steps of the hospital in Philadelphia.)*

Well, the sooner she started, the sooner she would make it to the top. If there was one thing she had learned in her fifty years of living, it was that—for her, at least—action generated strength to go on acting.

But before she could begin, she must know not only his name but what sort of man he was; whether he knew or cared that he had fathered a child; whether he cared for Millie, or used her to satisfy a lustful impulse, or seduced her simply for the sport of it.

She would know how to put her anger to use once she had an object on which to focus it. There were a few eligible bachelors in the community, but none who had shown any interest in Millie in the two years since she came down from Portland. Besides, a suitor of honorable intentions would have made himself known to the family...a married man, then? Harriet knew of at least three unhappy marriages in this end of the county. Any of these husbands might have turned to Millie for solace. (Solace was one of Millie's specialties.) But how could such a liaison have started? Millie lived like a recluse, only rarely leaving the farm to go into town, and never alone. The men who came to the farm could be counted on one's fingers: a few patients or spouses of patients, come to fetch the doctor; now and then an itinerant tradesman—butcher, knife-sharpener, some sort of peddler. Last summer, they had hired two hands to help with the stock, but neither of them would have had occasion to spend time alone with Millie—if she was ever alone. When Harriet was called to a patient, Millie went along to assist. Or did, until little Rogie came to live with them and she assumed responsibility for his care. Rogie took to Millie from the first moment he saw her. James said that when Harriet was away the boy followed Millie around like a puppy.

So when—in the past five months—could the wooing have taken place? Harriet had been gone only once—for the two weeks of the Medical Society meeting in Portland. James did not go up with her as he so often did because he was expecting guests—business acquaintances from the East. But they were gentlemen, not gypsies, and in any case, he would not have permitted them liberties with his foster-daughter.

On the other hand, what if James and his guests had gone on a day's excursion to inspect the land on which he hoped to build his golden rails, and someone had come knocking at the kitchen door to ask for directions or food or water: a drover on his way down the coast; an itinerant preacher; a seaman enjoying a brief shore leave while his ship took on supplies for the run up river or back out to sea. Millie would have answered the knock and given what was asked—but no more than that, surely! Even if Rogie had been napping or busy with one of his games, no stranger could have dismantled the wall of her shyness in the little time she would have been alone.

It was impossible. Simply impossible! Yet it had happened.

Millie had not been taken by force. (She would not have kept that sort of secret.) Someone must have made her believe that he loved her and would return for her, extracted a promise that she would wait for his return. Did she see herself as the heroine of one of the old ballads, waiting in patient silence for her true love's return? In the songs, the lover did return, sometimes to claim his bride, sometimes to weep over her grave.

Well, she could not be permitted to wait—not another month, not another week. If the man could not be found and brought to the altar, Millie would have to go away to bear the child, either to Portland or to San Francisco. Harriet had friends in both places who could help with the arrangements. Portland was more convenient, of course, but Millie was known to many people there as the doctor's ward and assistant, and Astorians often visited the city. San Francisco was a safer distance. But the distance created its own problems. Expense, for one. And could she get enough advance notice to be on hand to deliver the child?

"*There you go, Hattie! Rushing to meet trouble before it raises its head! Take care you don't bring it on that way.*" Mama's voice—or was it Sister's?—trying to bridle the impetuous filly she had been, and still was in many ways.

On the ride home, she began to rehearse the confrontation with Millie. There must be no overtone of anger or reproach that would cause needless pain, or worse yet, arouse resistance. Like many weak persons, Millie had a stubborn streak. Driven too far, she would set her heels like a mule and go deaf to reason. Tact was what was needed, and tact was not Harriet's strong suit. It would be better in some ways if she were to deal with the seducer and leave it to James to coax Millie into conformity.

James was a charmer, that was for sure. Handsome of face and carriage, courtly in manner, unquenchably optimistic, with an air of almost childish innocence. People forgave him his sins of irresponsibility, overlooked his shortcomings, made excuses for his blundering even when they suffered from it. It was just the other way round with her. People she had helped in their hour of greatest need sometimes turned against her. It was as if the heavier the debt of gratitude they owed, the quicker they were to find fault. To transform some inconsequential fault or inadvertent slight into a calumny, spreading tales that told more about the teller than the subject, if the truth were known. Of course, there were those who loved her more for her forthrightness—James among them. But even James had urged her more than once to try "catching flies with honey instead of a swatter." The trouble was that all too often, James failed to catch the fly at all. He was too vulnerable to manipulation—especially by his family—too trusting, too anxious to make himself liked.

It was not the first time she had wished their roles could be reversed.

The rhythm of Pride's canter was calming her anxiety and lifting her spirit. Or perhaps it was thinking about James, conjuring up his image, hearing and answering his voice. It still happened, despite all the ups and downs of their five years together, the joys and the sorrows, knowing that he had chosen her "to love and to cherish…forsaking all others," had made her young again, and beautiful.

As she started up the aisle of the church, he turned and smiled. Without the music of the organ to hold back her pace, she would have run to meet him. Without the familiar faces in the crowded pews, she would have doubted the reality of the moment. At her age, after the marital disaster she had survived! Everyone who knew her had been astonished. Some of those who loved her best warned her against it. She had listened to their doubts and fears—and bidden them to the wedding. There they sat—most of them—watching her walk slowly, steadily, toward a happiness greater than any she had known.

When they emerged from the church, there were people lining both sides of the street, cheering and wishing them well. She saw the faces of invited quests—some from as far away as Roseburg—and some who had not been invited—probably old patients or the relatives of patients. They shouted "Goodbye, doctor! Goodbye!" as the carriage rolled away. She waved and thanked them and promised to return.

They stood together to receive the congratulations of what seemed a multitude at the reception that was Ellen and Isaac's wedding gift. Her mother was there, and her two youngest sisters, Lyman, and the three youngest boys. Everyone but Papa and Sister, who must have been looking down from heaven and smiling, or weeping. James's father, old Colonel Franklin, did both as he leaned down to kiss her.

"Your father and I should be lifting a glass together! We talked more than once about which of our boys might take one of his girls, unite our two families." The rest of James's family were conspicuous by their absence. Mrs.

Franklin and both his brothers had been at the ceremony, but without their wives. (Was their failure to accept Ellen's invitation a snub directed at the bride, or the hostess, now Mrs. Isaac Rose?)

Then Aaron was standing before her, offering his "heartfelt wishes for as happy a future as you deserve." Patient, faithful Aaron, who had courted her for years, offering her his devotion and the security of an ample fortune, even the liberty to practice her profession. She had wondered sometimes why she could never make up her mind to accept that offer. But seeing him next to James put an end to the wondering. Worthy in every sense, Aaron was not a figure of romance. James looked the part of the prince who sweeps up his beloved and bears her away into the happily-ever-after.

Their honeymoon journey was like another chapter of the fairy tale, and its radiance did not fade when they came back to Portland: she to her medical practice and he to the pursuit of his great railroad scheme. When his affairs began to require him to be in Clatsop County for several weeks, she would take the steamer down and join him for a day or two, or he would take the steamer up and spend a weekend with her. Little by little, they settled into what seemed to many an odd sort of marriage, one that accommodated their two very different life patterns, granting freedom to each without loosening the bond of their love. They defended it, when challenged, by assuring the skeptics that short absences only made the heart grow fonder, renewing the joy of discovering each other. "Keeping love fresh!"

Disappointments and reverses of fortune came in time, but their love survived—even thrived on them...except for the last...that too would be outlived, but not soon.

※

There was no one in the barn, so Harriet could speak aloud what she had decided to say to Millie. She must begin very quietly, her words carefully chosen—neither provocative nor permissive—her manner straightforward, the tone of her voice warm, understanding, but not forgiving. She tried it several ways while she watered Pride and made him comfortable in his stall.

As she stopped to pull off her boots on the little porch outside the kitchen, she was seized from behind and nearly toppled. "G'amma! G'amma! Come see to Millie. She's took sick."

"What sort of sick, Rogie?"

"Throwing up sort," said the boy gravely. "She did it two times outside and once more on the stairs. But she cleaned it up before she took to bed."

Harriet poured the boy a glass of milk and found him some cookies, using the time to consider the significance of this news. Morning sickness? But it was late afternoon and months into the pregnancy. Had Millie taken something to rid herself of the child?

That was an alternative Harriet had not considered. But it was possible. If Millie had made that choice, perhaps the best thing to do was—nothing. Remain silent. Act as if she had suspected nothing.

But a new fear caught her like a cramp. What did Millie know about induced abortion? Harriet had treated one or two patients for ailments she suspected were the result of botched attempts to abort, but she did not remember ever having discussed the subject with Millie. To whom could the girl have gone for help? At best some Indian medicine woman; at worst some back-alley quack whose patients were waterfront whores. What if she had done herself irreparable injury?

One look at Millie reassured her on that score. The girl was not hemorrhaging, not in immediate physical danger. But if she had taken measures to rid herself of the child, they had failed. So the scene Harriet had been rehearsing must now be played. She spoke her piece—not badly, she thought—and waited. Millie had nothing to say. Her great china blue eyes were rimmed with red, and the expression in them reminded Harriet of the patient ox-like look she had come to hate in the eyes of some of the women who came to her to be healed, those who would go back to their abusers as soon as they were strong enough.

Harriet exhausted her own patience coaxing, cajoling, then demanding. Finally she lost her temper and said all the things she had promised herself not to—with just the result she had feared. Millie closed the portals of sight and hearing, retreated to some inner sanctum where no one—not even Harriet—could penetrate.

Watching from the kitchen window, she saw James ride into the yard, tie his mare instead of stabling her, and start for the house. He looked tired and dispirited, so unlike his usual self that she knew the interview at the bank had not gone well. It was a poor time to unload her troubles on him, but she had no choice.

He listened attentively, frowning and shaking his head from time to time, but saying nothing until she came had run out of words. Even then she had to prod him.

"Will you talk to her, James? See if you can persuade her?"

"To tell what happened?"

"And who is responsible."

James looked as if he were going to decline, but after another moment's silence, he shrugged and agreed to do his best.

"Explain to her that if he cannot be found and persuaded to marry her, she must go away to have the child. Unless she's done something to lose it."

"Done something? What do you mean?"

James's naïveté sometimes shocked Harriet, just as her blunt talk shocked him. She explained, as one might to an adolescent, the traditional—and the medical—methods by which a fetus might be aborted.

"But surely Millie would never try such a thing!"

"She may have tried already. It hasn't worked, but that's not to say it won't." And after he had gone, she found herself hoping that it would.

James's best was no better than Harriet's. Millie would not give the man's name, and she did not want to go away.

"She wants to have the baby here? Impossible!"

"Why?"

The simplicity of his question shook the foundations of her assumptions. For the moment she couldn't think of an answer.

"Who would be the wiser? People seldom visit here, and Millie always keeps to herself." James studied her face to see how much he was moving her. "After all, my dear, it's only a few months."

"And then? Afterwards?"

"We'll be as we were before."

"What about the child?"

"We could adopt him."

"And when your family asked who his parents were?"

That gave him pause, but not for long. "Why not say the mother was a patient of yours whose husband had deserted her? She died giving birth and begged you to keep the babe."

That was roughly the story of how she came to adopt Millie, but it could not be adapted to these circumstances. For one thing Millie's mother had not died giving birth; the scrawny little girl she had bequeathed to Harriet was almost five. There were neighbors who could attest to those facts (and who did not want to take responsibility for the child). And Portland was not Astoria. Gossip and rumor did not flourish in a city as they did in a small town.

"No, James, it's out of the question."

This time his "Why?" wrung an answer that surprised her. "Because—I cannot bear the shame."

James put his arms around her. Gently, lovingly, "But if you cannot persuade her…. How can you force her?"

She wrestled with the answer for days. James watched from a discreet distance, but made no further effort to intervene. Millie was back on her feet, doing her ordinary chores, but looking more than ever like a patient ox. The only member of the household who was not affected was her grandson, Rogie, whose high spirits and energy required—and got—responses from each of the troubled adults who populated his world.

By the end of the week, Harriet was resigned—though not reconciled—to Millie staying put and was beginning to deal with some of the decisions that would have to be made before things proceeded much farther. For one thing, Rogie, for instance, would have to go back to his father.

Harriet and James had taken her little grandson when his mother died. Meaning to raise him as their own, they had made him their legal heir. But last year Rob married again. His new wife was more than willing to have the child, but neither Harriet nor James had been willing to let him go. Now they would have to.

James saw how this pained her and tried to reassure her that it would only be for a few months.

Harriet shook her head. "Once Rob has him back, he'll never agree to let him go. Rogie is our heir, but he is Rob's son."

She saw James flinch and put her hand on his to comfort him.

They sat in silence for a while, then James said, "What an irony that fate should punish Millie with a gift that would bless us."

It was a thought she had been trying to dismiss for days. They had prayed so for a child—she, for a daughter, he for a son to bear his name into the next generation. That was something men set great store by. Women didn't—perhaps because they had no names of their own. Years ago, when she was fighting in court to regain the Ferry name after her divorce, someone had reminded her that it was Papa's name, not Mama's, and not hers.

※

"I've been wondering, my dear," James said to her one day, late in her pregnancy, "how you feel about naming the boy? James, of course, but he must have a middle name as well. Would you like him to bear your father's first name? Or his last? James Roger Franklin? Or James Ferry Franklin?"

"Whichever you prefer, my dear," she said. But it was not going to be a boy. Every fiber in her body told her that. A girlchild who would not have to strain against the shackles that had dragged at her mother's limbs, who would be given every advantage denied Harriet, educated and encouraged and inspired to become the finest physician the world had yet known. A girl who would become the woman her mother aspired to be.

The day that baby girl was born, James took her into his arms with loving tenderness that made tears burn Harriet's eyes even now. If his own expectations were disappointed, he gave no sign. They shared three days of euphoric happiness. Then, like a wicked fairy godmother who grants one's dearest wish only to snatch it away, fate took their perfect child. Stole upon her while she slept and stopped her breath.

Harriet fell into so black a depression that it was impossible to continue her practice. The voices of patients came to her as if from a distance, their words almost meaningless. She had to struggle to focus her attention on what they were telling her while her mind kept pulling back to that awful moment when she had stood beside the crib and looked down at that tiny face, pale as porcelain, beautiful and still…

One day Harriet opened the door of her waiting room to call the next patient, saw that it was a woman holding an infant, and began weeping inconsolably. She cancelled all other appointments and wrote to James that evening that she did not think she could bear up under this grief alone. "Can you not arrange your affairs so that you can join me here for a few months?"

James came up by the next steamer, but not to stay. He wanted her to close her Portland practice and come back down the river with him. "We need each other more than ever now, but I cannot leave my business."

His great venture had entered a critical state. The land he had purchased—with all of his capital and a considerable amount of hers—was tideland that must be reclaimed before tracks could be laid upon it. He had a crew of twenty-five Chinese laborers, working against the deadline of the oncoming rainy season.

"You can practice your profession anywhere, my dear. Once our clean, pure air has restored your health and strength, you can set up a practice on the Plains. And in no time at all—two years at the most—railroad trains will be running across our land, our fortune will be assured, and you will not need to work unless you wish to."

James had sold his home in Astoria and moved into a farmhouse on land he had acquired for his railroad. It was not far from the place Harriet's parents had homesteaded when they first came to Clatsop County. Her childhood home had disappeared without a trace, but the land had not changed, and as James had predicted, the ambiance had worked its healing magic.

Also as soon as she let it be known that she was available, there were calls for her services. It was not the sort of practice she was used to. Few of her patients came to her. Mostly she went to them—on horseback or by canoe—at all hours and in all kinds of weather. The nearest hospital was in Astoria, which could only be reached by ferry over the wide expanse of Young's Bay, or by a circuitous land route that led mainly through swamps. But the challenges gave her no time to brood, and although the climate was notoriously unfriendly to sufferers from arthritis, the regime of farm living was restorative to her general health.

In the end Harriet consented to the solution James proposed: Millie would remain at home. Harriet would deliver the child, which she and James would then adopt. Neither Rogie nor anyone else was to witness those events. As soon as Millie's condition became evident, she was to stay out of the way of all visitors—even Rob, who would be coming down from Yakima to fetch the boy. Nothing more was said about the matter of adoption, but she knew what James was thinking. Fate might be offering them a recompense. Nothing could replace her loss, but having Rogie about the farm had helped to heal them both. A child they called their own might serve as well.

II.

Millie was back on her feet and going about her accustomed chores, silent and unsmiling, keeping her eyes averted as if she was afraid they might betray what she was so inexplicably determined to conceal.

Without Rogie to splinter the silence, it locked like ice around Harriet's heart, but inside her head there was a din of voices—accusing, condemning, demanding explanations. Sometimes she wondered whether she had spoken aloud. Or whether she would ever speak aloud, freely, in this house again.

James's spirits seemed to lift as hers sank. His manner toward her was more affectionate and tender than ever, with overtones of something like gratefulness, as if her capitulation had been a favor granted him, rather than a recognition of necessity. And she was grateful to him—as always—for the protective shield of his love. Without it she wasn't sure she could have faced the strains of the coming months, much less the ordeal that would end them. Or would it merely replace them with other strains?

It was late in the spring to dig a garden, but work got her out of the house—out of Millie's way—and took her mind from the widening gap between them. The days were long, and she worked late into the cool, bright evenings, hilling seed potatoes and sweet corn, planting squash and turnips, and setting out cabbage seedlings. One more row and then she must stop or her back would give her trouble in the night. In the old days Millie would have offered to massage the soreness away.

She reached the end of the row and straightened up. A few yards away, just inside the thicket that bordered the cleared land, a doe stood like a statue, staring at her.

Harriet chuckled. "Planning your menu, are you?"

As the doe continued to stare, something stirred in the brush behind her. Two fawns poked their heads through the screen of berry bushes. Three pairs of eyes locked on to Harriet's. The silence pulled so taut it constricted her breathing.

Then the doe's ears flickered. The fauns turned their gaze from Harriet to their mother. Harriet's hearing wasn't sharp enough to catch the sound that alerted them, but as they vanished —dissolving like an illusion—James's voice called her name.

"Ah, there you are, my dear! I've been looking all over the place."

She could tell from his face that what he had come to say was not pleasant. (She had grown to rely so on James's unvarying cheerfulness that even the slightest trace of distress set off alarms.) "What is it? What's wrong?"

But he would not say until they had walked to what he called their reviewing-stand, a bench built at the edge of the bluff on which the house stood. When the weather was fine, they sometimes rested there, looking out over the panorama of pasture, tideland, and river beyond which the hills rose in long, low, blue waves to the crest of Saddle Mountain. This was the wilderness that James would transform into a golden kingdom with the magic wand of his rails. James cleared his throat, sighed, cleared it again, and began: "I have not wanted to burden you with this, my dearest. And nothing but absolute necessity drives me to do so now. But matters have taken a turn which threatens all our hopes." He made a long tale of it, but the problem was simple enough: his brother, Cyrus, had persuaded James to cosign a note that would come due in less than a month. Cyrus had no funds with which to meet the payment, and no one else in the Franklin clan was able—or willing—to help.

"How much is the note for?"

James named a figure far in excess of their cash reserves.

"Well then, you'll have to tell Cyrus to look elsewhere."

"You don't understand, my dear." James added a detail he had managed to omit from his telling, "You see, banks require some sort of asset as security. Cyrus has none. So, as co-signer..."

He couldn't bring himself to say it, so Harriet did.

"You put our property up as pledge?"

James raised his hands and let them fall in a gesture that admitted guilt and begged for pardon.

"But you had no right to do such a thing! The property is as much mine as yours!"

He loosed another torrent of words, explanations that fell short of the mark, excuses he admitted were inadequate, finally an almost unintelligibly contorted admission that he might have—unknowingly—committed "what might be construed as a violation of the law."

Still too stunned to be angry, Harriet groped her way to the core of his confession: he had let the bank assume that the property was his to dispose of, her name was on the deed, but the loan officer had not asked to see it. If he had, her signature would have been required. If a foreclosure were ordered now, only James's half-interest would be affected, and the bank would be unable to dispose of it without her concurrence. But the resulting legal imbroglio would ruin him.

"Reproach me as you will! You cannot be harder on me than I have been on myself."

"What I can't understand is why you didn't confide in me."

"I had every intention. I wanted—needed!—your counsel. I came up to Portland to ask it. But you were too ill to be concerned with such matters."

It was true that there had been a few weeks—perhaps a month—right after the baby's death when that was the case. "Was Cyrus in so great a hurry that you couldn't wait?"

"Not on his own account…that is, not on his personal account. The fact is, as you know, Cyrus has been handling Mother's investments. It seems he has made some…," James tried and failed to find words that would deflect her rising indignation. "To be blunt about it, my dear, Mother's financial security was at risk."

Another strand in the tangle of Franklin affairs. After the old Colonel's death, Cyrus and young T. C. Franklin had persuaded their widowed mother to let them manage her estate. Ordinarily the responsibility would have fallen to James as the eldest, and he had been deeply hurt by what he took as a slur on his business acumen, but which Harriet suspected was one more expression of the family's hostility to her.

In either case, the choice had cost old Mrs. Franklin dearly. It had taken only two years for both Cyrus and T. C. to squander their own inheritance and to jeopardize their mother's. And James was too loyal a son to see his mother reduced to penury. The note he had cosigned was to regain title to a major piece of property she had permitted Cyrus to encumber.

Now Harriet, the despised wife, was being asked to rescue them all. James wanted her to mortgage what property she still owned in Portland to cover the debts of a family that even now treated her like an embarrassment. He could neither understand nor defend the Franklins' rejection of her, but he had never given up hoping that what he called her "wonderful goodness" would melt the ice in their hearts. (Perhaps that was another reason he found it impossible to resist their appeals.)

Harriet had no such illusions. She neither expected nor wanted their friendship. Like Shylock, she could have savored the revenge fate seemed to be offering. But if she refused to do as James asked, he would be bankrupt and disgraced. And the ruin that engulfed him would do the same to her. Without his railroad, her half interest in the land would be worth less than the sum she had invested in it; surely not enough to provide them a comfortable living.

Finally, there was a chance—slim though it might be—that if all went well, the railroad still might be built on land that was still theirs.

Within hours her of granting consent, the spring of James's optimism was flowing again: the first payment by the joint-stock company financing the project would pay off her mortgage debt; the prospects for an early ground breaking were improving; work on the tracks would most likely be started in the spring; and there was already talk of extending the line farther down the coast.

But Harriet no longer drank from that spring.

In her darker moments, she asked herself how she could have made the same mistake a second time. Not that they were anything alike—the men to whom she had entrusted her heart and her hopes. James was educated, traveled, knowledgeable in the ways of the business world—or at least, so she had been told by men whose opinion she respected. Will Ross was a rough frontiersman, handy with a rifle or a hammer, brave in the face of challenge, but quick to tire of sustained effort. James was unwavering in his dedication to his dream of empire. Will was not without ambition, but it shifted like clouds in a storm wind.

※

Her own ambition—the one that had propelled her into marriage in the first place—was independence; escape from the burdensome role of eldest daughter that fell to her when Sister married and started a family of her own. Hattie was younger than Sis had been—barely fourteen—but she was healthy and strong and smart enough to perform whatever tasks were asked of a pioneer wife. Will was a good carpenter, a hunter, and a hard worker. He had helped Papa drive the Ferry's herd from Clatsop to Roseburg, and Papa said he'd never hired a better hand. They had his blessing and the promise of whatever help they might need to start off on their own. There was no reason they shouldn't prosper as well as the Ferrys, who had started with less.

Hattie spent the winter before the wedding preparing for the home she intended to make. Mama gave her enough muslin to make sheets and pillow cases, and a flour sack full of dress scraps from which Hattie was able to cut pieces for four quilts. She had all but one of them finished by spring, when Mama cut out and helped her sew a fine new dress for the wedding. With the money she saved from selling the eggs of her little flock of hens, she bought dishes, two-tined forks, and a half-dozen German silver teaspoons. Papa's wedding gift was a saddle horse named Molly, two cows, and a heifer calf.

Will's worldly possessions were less impressive: a horse, a saddle, a gun, and a few dollars. But his credit was good enough to buy them a homestead of three hundred acres, within visiting distance of the Ferry place. Twelve of the acres were fenced and seeded for oats and wheat. There was a small log cabin, roofed with cedar shakes, but as yet without a floor or a chimney. It did have a two-paned window cut into one of the logs, and a door so low that Will had to stoop to come in through it. But it was enough to shelter them while they worked on their "real" house, using lumber bought on Papa's account.

Will knocked together a "pioneer bed" (built against a wall so that it needed only one leg), a table, and some shelves. Snakes and lizards had been spending winters in the empty cabin, using the cracks between the logs as their entrance and exit routes, so Hattie's first chore was to fill the cracks. Back on Clatsop Plains settlers had learned from the Indians where to find a clay-like soil that could be mixed with tree moss and ferns and would dry as hard as plaster. She searched along the river banks till she found a patch of clay that would do as well. By the time the cold nights drove the reptiles to seek shelter, the cabin would be sealed tight against them, and she would be free to help Will with the rafters of the new house.

By October they had the roof on and were starting on the floor. But before that was finished, Will decided to stop and work on the door. Before that was done, he smashed his left thumb so badly that he had to stop work entirely to let it heal.

That was when their troubles began.

The first of the winter rains discovered leaks in the new roof that dampened their bedding. With neither windows nor door and only half a floor, there was no hope of drying anything. Papa had found them a new wood stove, but Will hadn't got round to cutting a hole for the stove pipe, once they had the money to buy it. (Hattie had been saving her egg and butter money for that purpose, but she had only enough to buy half what they would need.)

There was nothing for it but to keep on using what passed for a stove in the old cabin. There were leaks in that roof, too, and with only a mud floor, the cabin was even colder than the unfinished house. But at least she could cook—when there was something to cook. Will's hand hadn't healed enough for him to go deer hunting, so most of what they had to eat came from Hattie's chickens and the fresh cow. But whenever she snatched time for a visit to her parents, there was a sack of good things set aside for her to take home.

On one of these occasions, Mama murmured that a man with a good right hand and a wife like Hattie to help him could have gone ahead and finished the flooring and hung the door.

"Should I say something to him, Mama?"

Mama thought a moment, sighed, and shook her head. "Best not. It most likely would only make things worse."

When Hattie returned to the cabin that night, Will was busier than she had seen him in weeks, bringing everything into the new house and getting ready to board it up. He had decided that they would "take ourselves and the cows and pay your folks a visit."

As she helped with the boarding up, it struck her that it was as much work as it would have been to finish what was left to do on the house. But she remembered Mama's warning and held her tongue.

The young couple stayed with the Ferrys for two weeks, at the end of which Papa bought pipe for the stove and a supply of groceries. He and Mama came back with them to help to install the stove and hang the door. Will finished the floor and put in the windows and Hattie's spirits soared.

At last she could spread her quilts on the new bed and the rag rug she had braided on the floor. The new windows needed curtains, and she was tempted to cut them from her wedding dress. (There would be few chances to wear it in what she could foresee of the future.) Both cows were fresh now, and what she earned from their butter and cream would buy all the groceries they needed through the winter. In the spring Will would clear more land for pasture and plow another ten acres for wheat. With what they got for the grain crop, they could pay off the rest of the house debt and have plenty left to see them through the next winter.

The worst was over. They were on their way at last.

But Will's family had other ideas. His father wrote urging them to sell out and join the trek to northern California where a new vein of gold had been discovered. Fortunes were there for the digging! But the news was spreading fast, and those who waited too long would find the best claims already snapped up.

Will caught the gold fever and Hattie had a touch of it herself. She sensed that Papa disapproved, but for once she was willing to cross him. If he spoke his mind, she was ready to speak hers.

Neither he nor Mama made any attempt to dissuade them. But selling out turned out to be more complicated than they had expected. The farm was not yet theirs. Half the purchase price was due in April and they had no money to make the payment. However, Will was a great one for bargaining. He talked to the former owner and persuaded him not only to take the place back, but to pay them a small sum for the improvements they had made. With that and what Hattie could get for her chickens, they bought a few things they would need for the journey and started out; Hattie mounted on her beloved Molly, driving their herd of two cows and a calf and leading another horse to be sold in California.

They stopped on the way so Will's mother could meet her new daughter-in-law. Mother Ross had only the one son, and she made no secret of her hopes for grandchildren. She looked Hattie over as carefully as if she were considering a purchase, sighed, and shook her head. "Looks to me like you're nothing but a child yourself!"

Hattie was highly offended. She was going on fifteen, strong as most men her age, able to do anything they could, not to mention one thing no man would ever be able to do.

By the time they set off on the final leg of their journey, she was almost sure she was pregnant. She said nothing to her mother-in-law, for fear she would be forbidden to ride any farther. There were times on the way when she wondered if she had been foolhardy, but her thirst for adventure (and her sure-footed mare) brought her through unscathed. What they found once they reached Yreka was harder to bear.

With the money from the sale of their wagon and all their livestock (except for Molly, with whom Harriet could not bring herself to part), they made a down payment on a one-room shack with a lean-to kitchen and moved into it just before the winter rains began. While Will spent his days sloughing up one creek and down another, searching for a promising claim, Hattie cast about for a way to earn food money.

For awhile she apprenticed herself to a seamstress who made shirts to order for the miners and had more work than she could handle. In a few weeks Hattie was earning enough for the two of them to survive on, but when the baby came, that income would cease. Will was getting discouraged and his temper was souring. They quarreled over the cost of Molly's pasturage, Will contending that the mare was not earning her keep. Hattie tried to persuade him to find work as a carpenter, at least until the weather improved enough to make prospecting possible.

In the end, he gave in—sulkily—and rustled up enough odd jobs to take them through the worst of the winter. Their son—a small, sickly baby whom they named Rob, for Will's grandfather—was born in March.

Hattie half-expected Will to go back to his search for a claim, but he seemed to have lost interest. Yreka was a boomtown. There was plenty of work for a man as handy as Will and the seamstress was willing to give Hattie some finishing work she could do at home. They were making out—not happy and not entirely healthy—when the Ferrys' wagon pulled up in front of their shack.

Papa and Mama and the two youngest children had driven over a hundred miles to see the new baby, and—though they did not say so—to see how the new parents were faring. Hattie thought she had never been so glad to see anyone in her life. But she was also nervous, knowing what they must be thinking, afraid of what would happen if Papa spoke his mind. For she had learned by now how wise Mama was when she warned that scolding Will would only make him angry and stubborn—especially if he knew in his heart that he deserved it—but both her parents seemed oblivious to the desperateness of their situation, their attention entirely focused on the baby and his precarious state of health. It was three days before Papa found an occasion to make Will a proposal. His tone was almost offhand, but his words made Hattie's heart pound. "Why don't you and Hattie ride home with us? Roseburg has grown since you left. A carpenter good as you should have no trouble finding steady work."

Hattie was holding the baby too tightly and he started to whimper. Will scowled in annoyance, but had nothing to say.

Papa went on, his manner still very casual. "It happens I've bought up some land across the creek. The boys and I are operating a ferry service and we needed a dock. You two can have an acre or so and the lumber to put up a house on it." (Not a word of reproach about what had happened to the lumber he had provided for their first home, which Will had sold off to raise money for the trek.)

Will accepted the offer as he had accepted all Papa's past generosities, as if it was no more than was to be expected, and set about winding up their affairs.

Once again the final payment on their dwelling was coming due, and they had no money. Once again the owner was glad to take it back, but this time Will was unable to wangle a payment for the work he had done on it. So they started back poorer than they had come, except for the treasure Hattie carried, wrapped in her shawl.

The journey north was not the grand adventure the way down had been. Neither Hattie nor the baby bore it well but with Mama to look after them and the prospect of a happy ending to their travails, Hattie was able to convince herself that this time all would work out for the best—once she was well enough to carry her share of the work.

Papa said Hattie was to choose their house site, and she picked one near the ferry landing, which made her feel closer to her parents and the security they represented. Her brothers hauled the promised lumber from the mill in town and offered to give Will a hand with the walls and the rafters. But Will had been persuaded by a friend to go into the business of burning brick. More animated than she had seen him in months, he set up a large tent to shelter her and the baby. Then he and his new partner set about building an oven and mixing their first load of bricks.

The enterprise proved more difficult than Will had expected, but he worked hard. By the end of the summer, the partners had produced a few hundred usable bricks—not enough for the house they had planned, hardly enough to sell for the money to make more. The autumn rains were early and heavier than usual. The first one brought the river over its banks and flooded the brickyard. Will had to move the tent to higher ground, but the rains continued and the river banks became saturated. All sorts of creatures, including snakes, were flooded from their burrows and sought sanctuary on the same knoll. Hattie's frantic attempts to drive them from the tent drained whatever strength she had regained.

Toward the end of October, she came down with typhoid fever and the baby caught it from her. Mama took them both to her house to nurse them.

It was a month before Hattie was well enough to manage on her own, and for the first time in her life, she had no heart for the prospect that faced her: going back to tent living with a baby who was still thin and colicky and a husband who had no patience with infants. (Will had given up on brick burning, but he had done nothing with the lumber, nor did he seem about to.)

Swallowing her pride, she confessed her despair to her mother. "It'll just start all over again: the baby crying, Will yelling at him to hush, and that only making him cry louder. If it were only for awhile—if things were going to be better—if I could do anything to make them better...but it's no use. I know it. And I don't see how I can stand to go back."

Mama's mouth tightened the way it always did when she was vexed, but determined not to say so. "As far as I'm concerned," she said, "this is your home whenever you want it to be. But you'll have to talk to your papa."

Hattie half hoped it might be easier than talking to Mama, but it was harder.

"You want to leave your husband? For good? You want..." Papa swallowed as if the word threatened to gag him, "a divorce?"

Hattie hadn't thought that far ahead. "I—just don't want to go back. And I don't think Will cares whether I do or not."

"Maybe not. But what about the boy?"

"He wouldn't want to keep Robbie. Besides, how could he? He never took care of him a day yet."

"What about his folks?" Mama asked. "Didn't you tell me his mother wanted a grandson to raise?"

It was true. Mrs. Ross had hinted broadly that she was in a better position to care for the baby, at least while Will and Hattie were "getting themselves established."

"Do I have to be divorced to make sure I can keep my baby?"

Mama said they ought to have a talk with Papa's friend, Lawyer Charlton. But Papa was unwilling to air their troubles before even so friendly an audience.

"There has never been a divorce in my family. I never thought there would be. The shame of it would..." He caught Mama's eye and left the sentence unfinished.

In the silence that followed Hattie could hear Papa's breath rasping in and out. It reminded her of something...another place, another time...maybe part of a dream. She tried to summon it back, but all that came was an odor—wood smoke, fresh-cut cedar, and the stink of uncured leather.

Mama's voice brought her back to the present, low and gravely with anger and indignation. "Can't make a living no matter how much help he gets from us—and from Hattie! He's got a bad temper and no one to take it out on but her and the baby. I tell you, Roger Ferry, if she stays on with him, one of these days he'll do something he'll be sorry for. And so will you!"

There were tears in Papa's eyes. He took Hattie's hands in his. "I beg you, daughter, go back and give it another try. The weather's turned fine. Will can get an early start on the building. The boys and I will help. I give you my word: you'll have you a house before winter sets in."

"You don't know him, Papa. He'll start all right, but pretty soon he'll want to take off to go hunting or prospecting or something else. I'll have to nag to keep him working. We'll start quarreling again and…" Now she was crying, too. "Mama's right. Will's got so it doesn't take much of anything to make him fly off the handle."

Papa took her in his arms. "All I'm asking is for you to try. Do your best to put on a cheerful face. Help him all you can, but remember your first duty is to yourself and your little son." Papa took a deep breath before he committed himself: "If it doesn't work out, if he raises a hand to you or the babe—I'll bring you home myself."

Will was not at the house site when Papa escorted her home, but he turned up that evening and seemed glad to see her. She made a good supper from the groceries Mama had sent along, but smoke from the wood fire drifted into the tent and made the baby cough. Twice in the night she had to get up to pacify him, and Will began to grumble that she was spoiling the child.

Next morning Papa was back to have a talk about starting on the house. Hattie stayed in the tent and tried not to listen, but in no time Will's voice had risen to where she couldn't help but hear.

"I've got no deed to this piece of land," he was saying, "and I'm not fool enough to start building on it without."

Papa's reply was icy. "Hattie's mother and I have talked the matter over and in view of the use you have made of our past offers—the straits to which you have brought your wife and child—we think it best to do what we can to secure their future. The deed is in her name."

Will was so angry she was afraid he would raise a hand to Papa. But of course he didn't. In his time as a sheriff, Papa had faced down men more dangerous than Will Ross. Her brothers said he had a look that would stop a runaway mule.

"Think it over, son," Papa was saying. "Don't make any rash decisions. As long as you do you duty by your wife and son, you may count on our support. But it will be on the terms I have explained."

As soon as Papa had ridden off, Will saddled his own horse and went off without saying where he was going. Late that night he came back and told

Hattie he had bargained for a lot in town. A friend was lending him a team to haul the lumber to it, and as soon as it was light, he intended to begin.

"We'll have us a house in spite of him and his terms."

Hattie managed not to say a word. She had promised to keep cheerful, help when her help was asked, and bend all her attention on regaining her health and the baby's, and she did her best to keep that promise. But she made little headway on either score. Sometimes it seemed to her that Robbie was losing ground. His appetite was good, but no amount of food seemed to put weight on him, and his colic had become chronic. He seemed thinner and frailer every week.

By the end of the first month, Will had put up the walls (except for one side of the kitchen) and roofed the whole house. The unfinished side of the kitchen—the one that was to have the door and windows—was still open when he moved her and the baby in. Hattie began cooking their meals on the new stove. (Papa had made good on his promise to help by providing them with groceries.)

But the kitchen was invaded every night by an army of skunks, who grew bolder and bolder, making a racket that carried through the thin partition and started the baby crying in his crib. Will refused to get up and drive them away, reminding her of the consequences of putting them on the defensive. Once the skunks had wakened him, Robbie didn't leave off crying till Hattie got up and walked him. One night when even that didn't seem to help, Will told her to put him back in the crib and come to bed.

"He'll stop his crying when he knows he's not going to get anything by it."

She did as he asked, but the baby's crying only got worse. Will got up and shook the crib so hard that the child was shocked into silence.

"Next time he decides to cut up you let me handle it. I'll spank the devil out of him for good."

"Spanking him isn't going to do anything but make him cry harder."

"We'll see."

It was only a few hours before that "next time" came and Will had not forgotten his threat. At the first sound of whimpering from the crib, Will jumped out of bed, forbade Hattie to interfere, and delivered a spanking—with the result she had predicted. She walked the floor with Robbie for an hour before the sobbing quieted, then nursed him, laid him back in his bed, and crawled, exhausted, into hers.

After a few more such experiments, Will became convinced that the boy's problem was not lack of discipline, but hunger. Hattie didn't have enough milk to satisfy him. It was time he had something solid to fill his stomach. Will boiled up a dozen eggs and announced that he was going to "let the brat stuff all he wants." Over her violent protest, he fed the baby one hard-boiled egg after another until only six remained. Hattie spent a sleepless night, terrified lest the child go into convulsions.

In the morning her temper flared as high as Will's. The quarrel started over something so inconsequential that afterwards she couldn't recall what it was. But in no time at all their voices woke the baby, and he started crying. Will picked Robbie up and shook him. Hattie tried to wrench the child from his grasp. Will struck her a blow that toppled her onto the bed. A moment later, the baby was thrown down beside her.

For a moment she thought Will had killed the baby. "He'll do something he'll be sorry for." This was what Mama had meant.

Robbie started whimpering. She breathed a little easier, but she didn't stir, didn't open her eyes. She was waiting for the next blow to fall. Would it be on her, or on the crying child?

At last the silence was broken by the thud of Will's footsteps. She opened her eyes. The hide that served as a door to the kitchen was still moving. Will had pushed his way past and was gone. The baby was crying hard now, and her head ached so that each cry was like another blow.

She struggled to her feet, pulled one of the quilts from the bed and wrapped him in it, threw another around her shoulders, and made her way down the path to the river, to the ferry landing. She meant to hide herself in a thicket close by till the boat came over to this side. But it was already there, tied up and waiting for passengers.

Her brother Lyman took her bundle from her and helped her aboard. He asked her no questions. In fact, he hardly spoke till he had tied up on the other side. Then tucking the baby under one arm, he picked her up with her other.

As he half-carried, half-boosted her up the steep part of the bank he said, "Seems like you're getting smaller every year. Or is it because I'm still growing and you've stopped?"

III.

By the end of September, Millie could no longer manage the milking, so Harriet took it over. It was a chore she had resented as a girl, but now she found it strangely comforting. Leaning her head against the cow's flank and closing her eyes, she could think herself back into the time when she had done much of her dreaming like this. Today something was leading her deeper into the past than usual—a familiar odor, or the memory of one: a blend of wood-smoke, freshly-cut cedar, badly tanned leather, and damp earth.

She had been awakened by voices—quarrelling in hoarse whispers on the other side of the wall The new baby began to whimper and Mama got up to nurse him. The whispering stopped, but the menace of the quarrel hung over Hattie and kept her from sleep.

It was different from the quarrels that rumbled between her parents whenever they thought they were alone. This was like one she had overheard long ago. Was it on the trek west? Or just before they started off? What were they quarreling about?

Little Hal snorted in his sleep and turned over, stirring a wave of leather smell from the hides that were laid over and under their pallets. There was silence on the other side of the wall, and Hattie began to weave a dream about tomorrow, as she always did when she wanted to sleep...

Papa had promised to make a puncheon floor when the rains slacked off, and she was going to help him. The older boys would be busy with the herd, and Hal was too little to be trusted with tools. But Hattie was not. She already knew how to drive nails, and Papa was going to teach her to saw.

Hattie was Papa's favorite. Mama said she was too much of a tomboy ever to make a lady like Sister. But Papa called her his "boy," and in his mouth the word sounded like praise…

The quarrel had started up again. Mama's voice sounded almost angry.

"I was already carrying the baby…wonder I didn't give out and die like poor Mrs. Dawson…But when you take a notion there's nothing and no one gets in your path without being trampled…"

Hattie was frightened. She had never heard Mama sound like that before. Her voice was rising so that it was bound to wake her sisters, asleep on either side of her on the hay-stuffed plank bed.

The sound of a slap. Then silence. And after a bit, the grunting noises she knew even then meant that her parents were copulating like the animals of their herd.

A hand laid on her shoulder startled her out of the dream. It was James. "I think you'd better come to Millie," he said. "She can't be in labor! It's too soon. Weeks too soon." But Harriet was already on her way.

Millie was lying in her bed, pale and frightened. Her water had broken, but as yet she had had no pains. It was going to be a hard delivery, not without danger to both mother and child. The possibility that she might lose them both cleared Harriet's mind of all other concerns.

After eighteen exhausting hours, she was able to claim victory: Millie was going to be all right, and so was her undersized, but otherwise healthy little son.

James's reaction to the announcement was not what Harriet expected. Not that she could have said what it was she expected: relief that nothing had gone wrong with Millie, of whom he was as fond as if she had been his own; anxiety over how their version of the event would be accepted by his family; or the same anguished envy Harriet was struggling to suppress?

All he said was, "I suppose we must make arrangements to have the child baptized."

"Not just yet. We'll let a few weeks pass. At least a month."

James turned his head away too late to hide the pain that flickered across his face. He had taken her words as a reminder of the child that did not live long enough to have a name. Explaining that she had only been thinking of ways to throw the local gossips off the scent would only wound him more. Try as she would, she would never achieve the kind of sensitivity that came naturally to James.

"You are quite right, my dear," he was saying now.

It was years before the subject was discussed between them again.

Not many days later, Harriet took a notion to red-up the downstairs, starting with the room James called his office. It had not been cleaned in months. Sorting through the accumulation of books, papers, letters, and bills that covered his desk, she came upon the Franklin family Bible, which was usually kept on a high shelf of the bookcase. The gold-fringed bookmark was inserted near the center, where births, marriages, and deaths were recorded. It occurred to her to wonder whether he had entered the birth of their daughter—and her death.

She opened the book and leafed through to the last page of entries. There was the date of their wedding: June 23, 1885, James Thomas Franklin took in marriage Dr. Harriet Frances Ferry in Portland, Oregon.

Then there was a blank line.

On the next—in James's hand—was recorded the birth of James T. Franklin, fourth in the line, on September 29, 1898.

She closed the book, dusted it, restored it to its usual place on the high shelf, and went on with her cleaning, working with more and more energy, whipping her thoughts to keep them from straying into the swamp, singing under her breath to drown out the voice of the monster that was rising from it. Everything went on as before. She was still doing Millie's chores as well as her own, grateful that they took her out of the farmhouse for most of most mornings. The worst part of the day was when the three of them gathered for meals. Conversation was so forced that silence was preferable.

James's affairs were keeping him away from home more than usual, but when he was there, he seemed his old self, cheerful and affectionate as always.

At least to her. Toward Millie his manner seemed more formal than it had been. After an absence he would remember to ask after the baby's health, but that was all. Harriet watched and weighed every word either of them spoke, every look that passed between them. But she learned nothing. Physically Millie was recuperating well, but she seemed oddly indifferent to her child. She fed him at the breast as impersonally as if she were a wet nurse. It was Harriet who bathed him and dressed him and comforted him when he fretted. And in a curious way, he comforted her. Once she heard herself call him Robbie, and for a moment she was back in the time when she held her own little, sickly son, and wondered where she would find the strength to raise him.

Barely eighteen years old, in broken health and virtually illiterate, she was a shameful burden to the family that had already given her more than she had a right to ask.

While Mama fed and nursed her and Robbie back to health, Papa had been dealing with Will, who was trying to sell his interest in the unfinished house and the as yet unpaid for land. As the deed was in Hattie's name, the sale could not go through without her consent. Papa told Will that she wouldn't sign until he had permitted her to reclaim the clothes, quilts, and other prized possessions she had left behind when she fled.

That accomplished, Will found a purchaser and his black mood lifted. He tried to persuade Hattie to come back to him. She refused. Another quarrel started. Papa had to order him off the place. At the height of the argument, Will let drop what was hardly surprising news: his newly widowed mother wanted her grandson to raise.

His words stuck and festered in Hattie's mind. One day, when she felt up to the ride into town, she paid a call on Papa's friend, Lawyer Charlton, told him what Will had said, and asked what she must do to be sure of keeping her son.

The lawyer's bushy eyebrows lifted, and he tilted his head to one side as he considered his answer. "Perhaps the best thing to do in your situation is nothing. After all, young Ross isn't asking for custody at this point. Given time enough, things may sort themselves out."

"I will never go back to my husband. Never!"

"I was not suggesting that, but…let me put it this way: time cools even the hottest temper. In a few months—perhaps a year—he may have no stomach for a battle over custody."

"It's not Will that wants Robbie. It's his mother. "

"So your father tells me. And that is another reason I advise you not to file a petition for divorce. As things stand now, if the matter of custody were in dispute, Mrs. Ross could argue that she is better fixed than you are to provide for the boy. Why not let sleeping dogs lie, at least until you recover your health, get on your feet, and can make some sort of plan for your future."

Hattie thanked him and readied herself to leave. Lawyer Charlton observed her with an amused smile. "Your father says you are not of the temperament to tolerate uncertainty or inaction. But there are times when haste makes worse than waste. What is it the poet warns us of? 'what a dusty answer gets the soul when hot for certainties in this our life.'"

38

Hattie took her time getting home, trying to make up her mind whether or not to take the lawyer's advice, before reporting on her visit to her parents. She knew Mama would support whatever decision she made, but she wasn't sure about Papa. He had said if she tried once more—really tried—and failed, he would offer her refuge. But the idea of a divorce in the family had horrified him. And he hadn't wanted her to talk to Lawyer Charlton, but he had gone and done it himself....

It was nearly suppertime when she opened the kitchen door and walked in on a quarrel. It wasn't just Mama and Papa. Lyman and Hal and Ellen were in it, too. Everyone stopped talking the moment she came in, so she guessed it was about her they were quarreling. No one looked at her and no one spoke.

Then Robbie started crying in the loft. Lyman grabbed his cap from its peg on the wall and pushed past her and out. Papa got to his feet as if he meant to follow, but he lost his balance and had to hold to the table to steady himself.

Hattie thought he'd been taken ill. She would have gone to help him but the look on Mama's face stopped her. Papa straightened, stood a moment, then wove his way to the door like one of the derelicts she had seen outside the saloons in Yreka.

He was drunk! Reeling drunk!

And the fault was hers. She had shamed him past bearing, and this was the result.

Robbie was crying louder. She went up to nurse him. When she came down, everyone was sitting down to supper. Everyone except Papa. There was silence except for eating noises and the clinking of spoons on china. Everyone seemed to be avoiding her eyes. Now and then she caught one of the younger children stealing a look in her direction, then looking quickly back at their plates. Mama's mouth was folded so tight it was a wonder she could eat. By the time the meal was over, Hattie's face burned and her eyes stung.

The next day Papa seemed his old self. Life went on as before. Her brothers and sisters no longer avoided her. They still begged for the privilege of rocking Robbie's cradle or riding him around the yard in the little wagon Papa had made them. Mama was still pampering and nagging her about putting on the weight she had lost. But Hattie no longer felt at home. Or rather, she no longer felt she had a right to a place in the family she had disgraced. There was no way she could undo the harm she had done, but she was resolved to do no more. Not even to seek the divorce that would free her from the fear of losing the one precious thing her marriage had brought her.

The best thing she could do for them all was to leave, take Robbie and go. But where? And how was she to earn a living for herself and her son? She was barely able to read or cipher. The skills she had were those of a pioneer woman. She could ride a horse, herd cattle, milk a cow, make butter and cheese, raise chickens, cook simple foods, patch quilts, do simple sewing, wash, and iron. There must be someone somewhere who needed and would pay money for such services.

Perhaps she ought to wean Robbie and leave him under Mama's care while she looked for a situation that would include room and board for both of them or one that would pay enough so she could afford to rent. But when she tried to imagine leaving Robbie, even for a few weeks, her courage faltered. What strength she had she drew from her child's dependence. If she lost him—even for a little while—she would be lost.

She was still casting about for a solution to her problem when one presented itself. Her brother-in-law, Frank Hammond, rode down from Clatsop to beg for her help. Sis was pregnant again and ailing. Could Hattie lend a hand with the housework through these last difficult months? Yes, of course she could bring Robbie with her. His Hammond cousins would be as glad of a new playmate—or plaything—as his Ferry aunts and uncles would be sorry to lose him.

Mama had tears in her eyes when she kissed them good-bye. "We'll expect you home as soon as Sister can spare you." Hattie nodded, but it was not a promise. She knew she would never come home again.

IV.

As long as she kept busy, she was able to hold the door of her mind shut against the horror that was trying to gain entrance. But as she lay waiting for sleep—and even after it had come—it overcame her. Bits and pieces of what she thought of as "evidence" swirled in her head, challenging her to arrange them into a pattern she could accept as the truth:

James had given the boy his own name. But that did not prove he was the father. He had never ceased to long for a son. She had never ceased to long for a daughter. If Millie's baby had been a girl, she would have been tempted to claim her as recompense for the treasure she had lost. But the temptation James had faced was of a different order.

He had found himself alone in the house with a woman young enough to give him what his wife no longer could. Well, not quite alone. Rogie was there, but the little boy went to bed early and slept like a log. And James had some visitors from the East, but they stayed only a few days. For most of the time Harriet was away, he had both motive and opportunity to transgress.

But he was not the sort of man who could force himself upon an unwilling woman, and Millie was almost pathologically averse to physical contact with men. Besides, she regarded Harriet as more than a mother, one who had rescued her from unspeakable suffering.

It was impossible to conceive of either of them committing an act of cold-blooded betrayal. But what if it was not cold, but hot-blooded? What would have happened if a sudden spasm of lust overcame James's scruples? How could Millie, naive and trusting as a child, have defended herself? All she could have done was hope and pray that nothing would come of it. And afterwards, when that hope had withered, where could she have turned for counsel and comfort?

Cut off from the mother she had leaned on for most of her life, she could only suffer her punishment in silence. Naming her ravisher would only have dealt another blow to the woman she had already wronged.

Then why wouldn't she go away to bear the child? It was so clearly for the best—for her, for the child, for the family she was disgracing. If Harriet had not lost her temper over Millie's stubborn silence, perhaps she would have listened…but James had also tried to persuade her, and she had still refused.

Or was it he who refused?

Perhaps the decision James reported was his own, made in hopes that Millie was carrying a male child, the heir he longed for, fourth in what he called "the line." (What would he have written in the Bible if the child had been a girl?)

Perhaps. Always perhaps. Nothing was proved or disproved. Her mind raced like a squirrel caged in a wheel, round and round a circle that led nowhere.

Sometimes she thought that the only way to keep her sanity was to confront them with her suspicions. Demand to be told the truth and face whatever consequences flowed from it. But what if the truth was that she had misjudged them? They would never forgive her. How would they go on with their lives?

Months before Millie's condition became obvious, Harriet had let it be known that she would no longer accept patients at the farm, but she continued to answer calls. Today she had visited a homestead on the Plains where a woman no older than she lay dying of a malady that could best be described as an exhausted spirit.

Harriet did what she could to rally her patient, urged her to consider her blessings: a devoted husband, children and grandchildren, a comfortable home—the reward of a lifetime of hard, honest work. It had no perceptible effect on the patient and only deepened Harriet's own depression. As she left the bedside, an inner voice mocked her: "Physician, heal thyself."

Six month ago she too had a comfortable home, a devoted husband, a fine, successful son, a loving foster daughter, a merry little grandson. Now, Rogie was gone. Her loved ones had become the enemies of her peace. The only warmth she felt in her home came from the child whose birth had blasted her happiness.

In no hurry to return, she let Pride set his own pace and find his own way. The trail he chose was not the one they had come by, but the horse was headed in the right direction, and the footing was good.

In one of the broom thickets that sprang up wherever a homestead had been abandoned, they came upon a bramble-covered foundation that looked as if it had once supported a wooden structure. She reined in and stared until her memory restored the original.

Sis's house! The home that had first welcomed, then rejected her. What little was left of it. Frank had remarried and moved away the year after Sister died. Someone had told her the house was rented, but the tenants must not have prospered. Settlers in this area were penny-wise and finished lumber was dear. Any structure left vacant was dismantled long before its materials had been rendered useless by the elements.

Sis had a fine, healthy baby girl, but she was not recuperating well. Frank asked Hattie to stay on until she got her strength back. "I'll stay for the summer, but come fall, I mean to start school in Astoria."

"Why would you want to do that?" Frank asked in surprise.

"I need an education if I'm ever to better myself. All the schooling I ever had was from the teacher that boarded with us one summer. Lyman and Hal and all the younger ones went to school in Roseburg, but by then I was fixing to be married."

"You might want to marry again," Frank suggested. "You're still young and pretty enough."

"Put my foot in that trap again? No, thank you! I'll not be beholden to any man. And I'll not spend the rest of my life bending over a washtub either."

When Frank was convinced that she was not to be dissuaded, he offered her a bargain: if Hattie would work through the rest of the summer, he would pay her fees at the Academy in the fall. He would even help her find a place to stay in Astoria if she would come back and lend a hand on weekends and holidays. Hattie was delighted with the arrangement.

Sis was not. She didn't come right out and say why she minded, but she made her displeasure clear in ways that made Hattie wonder if she was jealous. Not so much of the interest Frank showed in her problems as of the exuberant health she had regained since she had been with them, while Sis had been growing thinner and paler and weaker.

"If you're that set on schooling," Sis said to her one day, "you'd do better to go back home. Mama says the school in Roseburg is as good as any in the Territory, and you'd have nothing to do but study. Mama and the girls are keeping house, and they could look after Robbie as well."

Hattie said she'd think about it, hoping Sis would let the subject drop, but she didn't. A day or two later, she reported that there was a party getting ready to ride down Roseburg way at the end of the month. Good folk who'd be glad to see Hattie safely home. Mama had been expecting her before now. Hadn't Hattie promised her to come back? What was her reason for putting off her return?

Hattie could think of no way to answer except with the truth. "I can't go back. Mama knows I can't. I was shaming Papa so bad it was driving..." She hesitated, unsure how Sis would bear up under the shock of what she was about to reveal.

"You mean he's started up his drinking again?"

"What do you mean, again?"

Sis broke out laughing. "You didn't know? Come now! You were a grown girl when they had to pull up stakes and go south. What did you think was the reason for that?"

"To find better pasture, wasn't it?"

Sister laughed again. Anger was bringing color to her face and strength to her voice. "It was because Papa was caught getting drunk on the liquor he took from the Indians he arrested. If he hadn't cleared out, they'd have taken his badge away."

For a minute Hattie thought Sis's illness had affected her brain. No one had ever spoken ill of Papa. Not here in Clatsop or afterward in Roseburg. Everyone admired him. Even wrong-doers. People used to say when he was sheriff, he had a look that would stop a thief in his tracks. He did carry a pistol, but he never had to use it.

"If you didn't know, you're the only one," Sis was saying. "I expect it's because when things started getting bad again, you were too taken up with getting yourself married to notice much of anything. And soon after that you had troubles enough of your own.

"But you can take my word: if he's fallen back into his old ways, it's not the first time. Not by a long shot. He's done it before. And more than once."

Hattie wanted to stop her ears against her sister's voice or run away out of earshot. But her body had stopped taking orders from her mind. Sis was going on and on, piling up words that weighted down and threatened to sink the image of the father she had worshipped.

"That's why they left Missouri. Sold everything and set out to cross the desert and the mountains. It liked to kill Mama that trip did. But Papa had sworn he'd never so much as look at a bottle again. He was going to make a new, clean start in a new place.

"For awhile it looked as if it'd be all right. He stayed sober on the trip and while he was building us a cabin and clearing the pasture and settling us in. It was after they made him sheriff, he began to backslide. And awhile after that, before it began to show."

"How?" Hattie's voice came out in a croak.

"I can't say exactly, I never saw the signs. But some people must have because there was already talk about replacing him as sheriff. Men he was friends with came to warn him. They said the best thing was to move away before it came to that. Pull up stakes again and start over some place where he wouldn't have so much to live down.

"Mama didn't want to go. She didn't think it would do any good. Frank said she was right. (His folk were strong temperance people back in Kentucky.) He said the only thing that would help was if Papa faced up to what he was doing and took the cure. He wanted to tell Papa that to his face.

"But Mama said it would only make things worse. Frank tried to argue with her, but she said she'd be the one to suffer if he got Papa riled up."

Hattie must have looked as stricken as she felt because Sis reached out and patted her hand. "So just remember, Papa's got no call to complain about you shaming him. He's the one who's brought shame on the family."

Hattie had decided—mostly for Papa's sake—to take the lawyer's advice and put aside, or postpone indefinitely, the notion of filing suit for divorce, but the question of custody still nagged at her. As long as Will didn't know her whereabouts she was relatively safe, but sooner or later he would find her—or his mother would—and the battle over Robbie would begin.

No longer bound by obligation to Papa, she asked Frank to write a letter to Lawyer Charlton saying she'd made up her mind: she wanted a divorce, custody of her son, and the right to reassume her maiden name.

At first Frank was reluctant. He and Sis had been hoping that what they took for a separation would lead eventually to reconciliation. But when Hattie had told him about Will's abuse, not only of her, but of Robbie, he agreed that she had done right to leave. But to sue for divorce, that was something else. It carried a stigma that would be hard to erase. Why not leave things as they were?

"Because Will's already tried once to get me to come back. His mother will see to it that he tries again. And as long as we're married, he's got rights as a father. She wants the baby, and she might go to court to get her way."

In the end Frank did as Hattie asked. After the letter was mailed, he mentioned it to Sister and she had a fit. She carried on about how she wouldn't be able to hold her head up in the county. People were beginning to ask if Hattie had come up on a visit, or left her husband, and if so, why? When they heard she was going to court for a divorce, decent folk would have nothing more to do with her. Her disgrace would punish the kinfolk who had held out their hands to help her.

Frank tried to comfort Hattie, assuring her that Sis didn't mean half what she said. "She hasn't been herself since the baby came." And before the day was over, Sis said the same thing. She didn't know what had gotten into her. She just hoped Hattie could forgive her and forget.

The sisters embraced, wept a little, wiped their eyes, and tried to go on as if nothing had changed. But Hattie had made up her mind to leave as soon as she could find a place to stay and enough work to pay the rent and buy food and what little clothing she and Robbie would need.

Pride stopped, snorted, and tossed his head. He had started on while she was dreaming. Now he had come to a fork in the trail. The way home lay to the right. To the left lay the sea. He was asking which way she wanted to go.

She turned him toward the sea.

She had the sense, that the reverie from which he had roused her had been leading toward some revelation, that if she picked up the dream where it had been broken and followed it far enough, she would come upon a certain, not a dusty answer, to the questions that tormented her. She must have time to think uninterrupted. There was no better place to do that than the hollow where she had hunkered down and watched the beetle climbing the hill of sand.

V.

The sands of the shore dunes had shifted. The hollow where she had sheltered in October was exposed to the wind blowing down the jetty. But on the landward side of the dune there was a thicket of shore pine and broom that promised some protection. She tied Pride's reins to one of the stouter trunks, tunneled into the brush, drew her knees up under her cloak and hugged them, closed her eyes, and waited for her mind to pick up the trail of memory where it had been broken off.

But her mind had a mind of its own. It went darting off in first one, then another, direction, exhuming bits and snatches of quarrels (most of them recent), slurs and snubs (mostly at the hands of James's siblings)—a medley of annoyances and frustrations that threatened to lead her away from, not toward enlightenment. Then quite suddenly, she was reliving one of the most stressful days of her life.

It was a Saturday morning, six months after she returned to Roseburg with a degree from Philadelphia's Eclectic School of Medicine. She did not keep office hours on weekends, but as she lived in rooms above the office, she heard the knock at her front door and came to answer it.

On the doorstep stood a boy she did not remember having seen in the neighborhood. "You the lady doctor?" he inquired. Harriet nodded. He grinned broadly and handed her a message, hastily scrawled on a page torn from a doctor's book of prescription.

"You are invited to attend the autopsy being performed on the body of the late Whiz Dubbins. Place: the shed on town property adjoining the Umpqua River Road. Time: now."

There was no signature, but the writing looked familiar.

"Who sent you with this?" she asked.

"The docs."

"Which doctors?"

The boy went through an elaborate pantomime of recalling. "Well, let's see now! There's Doc Gardner...and old Doc Palmer...Doc Hamilton's there, too...I reckon they all are. Folks say every doc in the town has took care of the old bum one time or another, so they all want to know what finally did him in."

"Do they expect an answer?"

"They didn't say. But I'm going back that way, so if you got one, you could send it by me."

His grin was so impudent that she wanted to slap him, but she maintained her dignity and said, "You may give the doctors my compliments and tell them that I'll be there directly."

The grin disappeared. "You're going out there and watch them cut him up?"

"Doctors are trained to officiate at such procedures and I am a doctor."

As she shut the door in his face, she heard the urchin mutter, "A bath doctor. Not a real one."

That opinion was shared by most of the citizens of Roseburg. Harriet's degree from the Eclectic School of Medicine qualified her in a limited number of procedures only one of which—a therapy involving electric baths—had so far attracted enough patients to constitute a practice. But even that small degree of success had outraged the medical establishment. She expected opposition from Dr. Palmer, who had been her enemy ever since the day she rebuked him for his clumsy handling of a child patient. But some of those who had used her services as a midwife or practical nurse were now openly hostile. The rest simply ignored her existence. Even Dr. Hamilton, who had once befriended and encouraged her, was no longer cordial.

If she had any illusions that the invitation was a signal that she was at last accepted into the priesthood, the boy's impudence would have dispelled them. She was expected to refuse, thus confirming their assumption that no female could or would face up to the more distasteful aspects of the profession. Their note was a gauntlet flung at her feet. She could retreat like a coward, or pick it up and prepare to fight.

When she pushed open the door of the shed the astonishment on the faces of the six men present was so comical that she had to struggle not to smile.

She greeted each of them by name, thanked them all for extending this "professional courtesy," and waited for whoever was in charge to respond. Everyone looked in the direction of Dr. Palmer but he seemed to have lost the power of speech. Finally someone she did not know (he must have come to Roseburg during the year she was away) cleared his throat and warned her that the autopsy would involve the genital organs of the deceased.

"One part of the human body should be as sacred to the physician as any other," she replied, trying to replicate the sententious tone of the anatomy professor who had opened all of his lectures with that pronouncement.

At this point, outrage restored Dr. Palmer's voice. If a woman was to be witness to the autopsy of a male cadaver, he would not stay to see it!

"What is the difference between a woman attending the dissection of a male cadaver and a man attending the dissection of a female, which you do all the time?"

No one had an answer to offer.

Harriet continued. "Was Dr. Palmer's objection not raised and discussed before you issued the invitation?" She looked at Dr. Hamilton but he was avoiding her eyes. "In any case, having been invited—I presume by at least the majority of those present—I will leave only when asked to do so by the same majority."

There was a full minute of unbroken silence.

"Well, I voted for her to come, and I'll stick by it," said one of the new doctors in town. Another said he would not go back on his vote. Two more reluctantly followed suit. Dr. Hamilton spoke last.

"I didn't vote on the invitation, but I have no objection." That made five out of six.

Dr. Palmer picked up his bag and put on his hat. As he left the shed, he was greeted by the cheers of a small crowd, which had assembled since her arrival. The grinning boy must have spread the news, and citizens of both sexes were gathering to see the lady doctor get her comeuppance, or the reverse.

Harriet considered that she had won the first round, but her opponents were not ready to concede the match.

The new doctor who had spoken first had been preparing to make the first incision when she arrived. Now he offered his medical case to Harriet. "If you have not brought your dissecting instruments with you, let me offer you the use of mine."

"You don't want me to do the work?"

"Oh, yes indeed." And he pointed to the operating table—a rough plank supported by two sawhorses—on which lay a still figure covered by a thin gray blanket.

Harriet was aghast.

She had never witnessed, let alone performed, a dissection. Such things were not part of the curriculum of the Eclectic School of Medicine, which claimed to draw its precepts from the competing schools of homeopathic and allopathic medicine, but which leaned perceptibly in the direction of the former. But she would not give these ghouls the satisfaction of having to revive her from a faint, so she forced herself to breathe deeply and regularly, walked to the table, pulled back the blanket, and went to work.

Bulletin after bulletin was issued in whispers to the watchers outside and transmitted by the grapevine to all parts of the town. By the time she was finished, the street was lined with men, women, and children, all eager to get a look at the woman who had dared to defy the customary decencies.

She walked past them, head held high by a poker-stiff neck, keeping her step firm although her knees were threatening to buckle under her. The hostility was so palpable that she wondered if a tar-and-feather party was in the making.

Her brothers Lyman and Hal knocked at her door a few hours later and announced that they would stay until she had made up her mind what she was going to do. A short while later, Ellen and Isaac arrived, and with them Isaac's partner, Aaron Weiss.

Ellen spoke for the Ferry family: while there were differences of opinion on Harriet's response to the doctors' provocation, everyone agreed that it would be impossible for her to keep a practice in Roseburg under the circumstances. Even people who had supported her in the past were scandalized by this exploit. Few, if any, of the patients she had acquired in the months since her return would continue to use her services, and no new ones would be knocking at her door. "If you try to stay on, you'll lose everything you've put into the office. All your hard work and sacrifice will be wasted."

They were also all agreed that the way out of this impasse was to pack up and move to Portland. "Chances are no one up there will hear about what happened, or care much if they do. You could put an advertisement in Mrs. Duniway's newspaper. Some of her readers will remember you from when you used to write for it." Ellen paused to give her a chance to comment, but Harriet could only shake her head. "Look at the bright side, Hattie. There's more opportunity in a city than a little town like this. Why, it may be you'll have yourself a bigger and better practice in Portland than you could ever have had here."

Everything was being decided for her: all the arrangements made by others. Ellen would see to her ticket. Isaac had looked up the railroad schedule and reported that there was a northbound train day after tomorrow morning. Lyman and Hal would crate all her office equipment and drive it to the depot. Isaac would see it safely on board. All Harriet had to do was to pack her personal effects. She made no objection.

The afternoon had drained her. It was all she could do to keep from crying in front of all her nearest and dearest who could not conceal their impatience to be rid of her.

Except for Aaron, who stayed behind after the others had left to ask her once again to do him the honor of becoming his wife. He had intended to propose as soon as she returned from Philadelphia, but remembering what she told him before she left on that journey, he thought it better to wait till she was established in her new profession.

All she could say was that he must still wait for that day.

"But Portland is not as far away as Philadelphia."

VI.

The last time she had refused Aaron's offer of marriage was the day she told him of her plan to close her business in Roseburg and set off across the continent in search of the degree that would qualify her to practice medicine.

He had been her faithful admirer ever since she moved back to Roseburg nearly ten years before. His partner Isaac Rose was married to Harriet's favorite sister and on one of his business trips Isaac paid her a visit in Astoria, explaining at the outset that he had been commissioned by Ellen's family to persuade Harriet to "come back home."

He could not have chosen a better time for such a mission. Harriet had fulfilled the ambition that had possessed her even before she could put words to it: she was independent, responsible only to herself, mistress of her fate. Her financial future was secure. A successful grade school teacher could always find a position on one side of the river or the other. The salary was modest but she had been able to save enough from it to have a snug little cottage built on the back of a lot near the Customs House.

One of her first visitors was Will Ross. She had received several letters from him in the years since their divorce, saying that he had settled down since inheriting his parents' spread and was "doing well enough to provide for you and our boy." She had not answered any of them and he had finally come to make his plea in person.

He had not expected to find her so comfortably situated, so much in command of herself and the interview. The admiring amazement on his face as he looked over the house and its furnishings was the sweetest of revenges. But it was also cause for alarm.

Under the terms of the divorce, Will had a right to visit with his son at more frequent intervals than he had been in a position to arrange, so when he asked if he could take the boy into town with him for a day, Hattie knew she could not refuse. But as soon as the two of them were gone, she got worried and paid a call on the sheriff.

"Mr. Ross threatened more than once that if I wouldn't be reconciled with him, he'd make off with Robbie and I'd never see either of them again!"

The sheriff patted her hand and assured her that Ross would never get out of Clatsop County with the boy. She had nothing to worry about on that score, he said. But even after Robbie was safely home that night, she went on worrying. What about the next visit? There were ways out of Astoria that would be hard, if not impossible to block. By water, for instance, up the Columbia or out over the bar. And she knew what Will could do when he was thwarted in a plan that was dear to him. Sister was dead and Frank was gone and she had no near neighbors. The prospect of living within calling distance of her loyal and pugnacious brothers was more appealing than it would have been a month ago.

Also, she was discovering that the teaching profession offered no prospect of advancement, nor any greater challenge than a succession of particularly unruly pupils. Isaac's talk of new and lucrative careers open to women fell on listening ears.

"Take millinery, for example. This last year we've made two buying trips to San Francisco and one to Portland looking for kinds of merchandise our customers are asking for. It's only a matter of time before someone opens a shop in Roseburg and whoever does will make her fortune in short order." He was prepared to back his opinion with the capital to set Harriet up in business. "And Ellen has charged me to remind you that your mother is much alone since your father's passing and misses you sorely."

It took Harriet only one sleepless night to decide to accept Isaac's proposal to pull up stakes as soon as she could and embark on a brand new career. It was years before she understood that what drove that decision was not only the prospect of a reunion with her family and a more ample income, but also—and perhaps more importantly—the prospect of returning to the scene of her youthful failures as a woman of accomplishment and means.

Isaac and Aaron made good on all their promises. They lent her the money to lease a small building on Roseburg's busiest street and convert its ground floor into a combined shop and workroom. On the second floor there was a small apartment where she and Robbie could live in reasonable comfort. On one of his buying trips, Aaron secured the tools and materials she needed at an excellent price. And her sister Ellen—now one of Roseburg's most affluent matrons—recommended the new shop to all her acquaintances.

But in the end, Harriet knew that the fate of the enterprise would depend on her ability to master a profession she had practiced only as an amateur and only for the last two or three years. As life became less stressed and her social position more stable, she had developed an interest in and a talent for feminine fashion that was surprising in one who had been such a tomboy in her youth. By the time she arrived in Roseburg, she was, by that community's standards, a "classy dresser," a walking advertisement for her wares.

As soon as she had unpacked what few possessions she brought with her and enrolled Robbie in school, she set about learning her new trade by disassembling some of the out-of-date millinery stock in Isaac and Aaron's storeroom and remaking them in styles copied from illustrated ladies' magazines. The results might not have impressed a sophisticated shopper, but they delighted Ellen's friends. The word of mouth spread their enthusiasm over the whole of Douglas County.

Harriet worked hard—as always—and success came early and easily.

Then one day toward the end of the second year, handbills appeared all over town announcing the opening of a millinery "atelier, featuring the latest Parisian and Eastern fashions in ladies' headgear." Gossips reported that the new milliner was a native of New York who had traveled in Europe and that she was making malicious fun of Harriet's "out-of-date" models and amateurish workmanship.

Business fell off sharply.

Harriet consulted her mentors, Isaac and Aaron. Both took a gloomy view of the situation. Roseburg was growing fast, but it was not yet large enough to support two millinery establishments. It would not take long for one competitor to drive the other out of business.

That was when Aaron first asked her to marry him. He had long admired her, he said, but hadn't dared to declare himself, seeing her so taken up with problems of launching the new venture. But of late he observed that her interests were widening and that gave him hope. What emboldened him now was what appeared to be a crisis in her affairs, but which might prove a blessing to her as well as to him.

If she would do him the honor of becoming his wife, it would be his greatest joy to provide for her and her son, leaving her free to pursue whatever cause or causes she cared to. And finally—with extreme diffidence—"Although I am no longer young and have never been handsome, I know myself capable of deep and lasting affection." Even this stiffly formal little speech cost him an effort that brought sweat to his forehead. He dabbed at it with a handkerchief and muttered an apology for his inability to express himself.

Far from being put off by it, Harriet found his struggle with words disarming. Also, though he was certainly no Apollo, he was by no means unattractive either physically or as a personality. Born in the eastern United States, he had traveled widely before coming west to make his fortune. Though he was considerably more cultivated than most of Roseburg's citizens, he was careful to hide his light under a bushel of modesty and as a result was universally esteemed. Indeed, according to Ellen, he was considered a "catch" by most of the unattached females in that part of Oregon. But he had never shown a serious interest in anyone—until now.

Harriet was flattered and touched. But she was not ready to commit herself, or—and this was what mattered most—willing to retreat in the face of the enemy. She refused him gently, even affectionately, but firmly.

Aaron accepted the verdict as if he had expected it and changed the subject to her professional problem. In his opinion, she ought to bite the bullet: acknowledge her lack of expertise, go to San Francisco, apprentice herself to an established milliner, and learn the trade from the bottom up. He had friends and business acquaintances in the city. He would ask one of them to recommend a suitable firm and arrange for Harriet to be employed in it. Her own shop could be left in the care of one of her younger sisters, and Robbie could board with Ellen and Isaac.

Isaac, who had tactfully absented himself from the first part of this discussion, agreed wholeheartedly with the plan. So did Ellen. Everything fell into place as if it had been preordained. Within a month, Harriet was ready to set off for the City on the Bay, the commercial and fashion capital of the West.

She spent a little less than a year at her apprenticeship and returned to Roseburg with new models and new confidence.

In six months she had run the competition out of town. A year later she moved out of the apartment above the shop, which was now enlarged and remodeled to accommodate the first show window in the area.

Harriet purchased a house almost as large as her sister's with a flower garden in front and a vegetable garden in back. The "other interests" that Aaron had observed were taking a larger and larger share of her time, in particular the struggle for women's suffrage. Harriet was Douglas County's first subscriber to Susan B. Anthony's feminist newspaper, The Revolution. Since her return from California, she had also subscribed to an Oregon suffrage journal called The New Northwest. Its publisher, Mrs. Abigail Scott Duniway, solicited articles from reader and two of Harriet's had appeared in print. The issue that included the latter of them also announced a series of lectures by Miss Anthony to be given in Portland.

The trip from Roseburg to Portland took two days by stage, and Harriet was in the process of convincing herself that she could justify the expenditure of time and money by using the days between the evening lectures to make the rounds of suppliers' shops, when she received a telegram datelined Eureka, California:

"SECURE ME A PLACE TO SPEAK SATURDAY EVENING. —SUSAN B. ANTHONY"

The telegram was delivered on a Friday morning. Harriet had less than twenty-four hours to secure not only hall, but an audience. There were only three buildings in the town with public rooms capable of holding as large a crowd as Miss Anthony merited. The biggest was connected to one of Roseburg's saloons. The newest was in the Court House, but that seemed hardly more appropriate. That left only the largest of the town's churches. Harriet was not sure about the minister's views on women, but he was an outspoken advocate of temperance and so was Miss Anthony.

She paid him a call, showed him the telegram, and asked if he didn't think the lady ought to have a church to speak in. He looked as if he were terrified of the probable consequences but couldn't find words to cloak his cowardice. Harriet chose to take his silence as assent.

"Then since your church is not only the biggest, but the best, I hope we may have permission to use it."

Before the man found a way to deny her request, she had thanked him and hurried away to pay a call on each of the trustees. None of them was any more enthusiastic than the minister, or any braver about facing her down. She gave them no time to caucus and reconsider, but went at once to the printing office and had several hundred posters made and paid a boy to put them up in every possible place in town. By the time darkness fell, all over town men were holding street corner debates on the significance of this extraordinary event.

Late in the evening the saloonkeeper whose hall she had considered stopped in at her shop to warn her not to expect much of an audience. "We're getting up a free dance and supper tomorrow, starting about an hour before your shindig." He didn't mention free drinks but Harriet knew how saloonkeepers usually operated to influence public opinion. On election days—particularly those in which their interests were directly affected—he and his competitors cooperated in an orgy of "hospitality" that reduced half of Roseburg's electorate to a state of helpless intoxication. They would do the same tomorrow.

She had been outmaneuvered, but it was too late to change her plan. All she could do was stay the course, hoping that Miss Anthony's reputation would draw at least a respectable handful of the converted and the curious.

When the tall, gray-haired, unexpectedly handsome lady stepped down from the California stage the next afternoon, only Harriet stepped forward to greet her. But there was a sizable crowd of onlookers, neither cheering nor jeering. It was hard to know whether the omens were favorable or ominous.

For the next two hours, while her visitor first rested and then prepared her toilette for the evening, Harriet debated whether or not to explain the opposition's tactics and warn her of the effect it would probably have on the audience. But when Miss Anthony came downstairs she hadn't the heart to say a discouraging word. The Quaker gray traveling suit had been replaced by a simple but elegant blue silk suit with a white lace fichu at the neck. The severe gray coiffure was hidden under a neat little bonnet with a dotted lace veil that Harriet would have been proud to have in her show window, and the pale serene face was flushed with excitement that took years from its owner's appearance.

When they started for the church (well ahead of the appointed hour because Harriet had the key to the entrance door), the advertised free entertainment was already under way. Windows on the ground floor of the saloon were open and through them came loud strains of music, the thud and tap of dancers' feet, and the slightly bibulous laughter of what sounded like a very large crowd indeed.

Harriet tried to keep up a line of bright chatter to deflect her companion's attention but Miss Anthony was not fooled. "Do not be disheartened," she said, patting Harriet's shoulder. "Those who are open to our message will not be diverted. Our task is to give them heart to carry it into places we cannot reach." When they turned the corner and started up the hill to the church, a different sound greeted them—the murmur of several dozen couples who had arrived well ahead of time and were impatient to be admitted. By the time Harriet ascended the platform to introduce the speaker, the church was half full. Some of those whose faces she recognized were certainly open to the famous suffragist's message, but there were others whose minds she would have expected to be closed and nailed shut against it. All in all, it was an audience to make the heart of an evangelist rejoice.

And Miss Anthony was inspired. Harriet had long admired and tried to emulate her writing, but she was not prepared for the eloquence of her speech. It was as if this quiet, composed, essentially reasonable person became, for the moment, the instrument through which a passionate spirit pled its cause. The power that possessed her was contagious. Harriet was not the only one of her listeners who caught fire, convinced that they too were invincible. Anything—everything they desired was within their power to grasp.

She could hardly wait to make her guest comfortable before the grate fire in her little parlor and to talk about what had been till now her secret ambition: to become a doctor—a real one—with a medical degree. Like most pioneer women, her mother had practiced frontier medicine and had passed the acquired knowledge on to her daughters. Of them all only Hattie had a natural turn for it. Since coming to Roseburg, she was often called upon to minister to women who couldn't afford or were afraid to consult a physician. Apparently she was gaining a reputation as a healer for of late, local doctors had begun asking her to assist them in certain types of medical emergencies. This experience had convinced her that, untrained as she was, she was as capable as most of them, more capable than some.

"Not long ago I was helping a friend with her sick child when old Dr. Palmer called upon her. His hand is quite shaky and he was trying to insert a catheter, causing the poor little sufferer so much pain by his clumsiness that I finally took the instrument from him and inserted it myself."

Did Miss Anthony think the healing art had been reserved by the Creator for his male children only? Miss Anthony did not. Members of the Society of Friends had always hoped that God did not discriminate between His children in any significant way. In this case, it was her opinion that a woman's life experience was better preparation for a medical vocation that that of the average man.

"It is true that women are on the average lacking in gross physical strength, but I am told that is seldom called upon in ordinary medical practice. On the other hand, we have a superior ability to endure long periods of strain and that may well prove of greater usefulness."

"But how are we to get the education we need? Dr. Hamilton, who lends me his medical journals, says he knows of no medical school that admits women."

Miss Anthony sighed and shook her head. Some eight or ten years earlier two medical schools in New England admitted a few highly talented and qualified women. But although these precedent-breakers graduated with honors and went on to do useful and important work in their fields, the same doors were now shut against women who aspired to follow them.

"The only institutions that do not exclude women at present, as far as I know, are the homeopathic and eclectic schools and their degrees are not recognized by the American Medical Association, which is allopathic in its approach.

"My friend, Dr. Joseph Longshore—who is also a Friend, by the way—is the head of Philadelphia's Eclectic School of Medicine. He believes in liberty of conscience, in therapeutics as well as in religion, and I know he has taken on female students he judged to be qualified."

"Would he consider me qualified? I could leave my business in my sisters' hands for a year or even two. And my son will be going to college in California this coming fall. I would undertake the journey gladly, if I knew I would be admitted."

Miss Anthony could not say whether Harriet's credentials would fulfill Dr. Longshore's requirements. "I should imagine that what you lack in formal education is outweighed by your experience. But there would almost certainly have to be some sort of examination."

"And I would have to go to Philadelphia to be examined? It's a long journey to take on the chance."

There was a long Quaker-silence while Miss Anthony weighed the probable consequences of the advice she was being asked to give. At last she said, "It would not be friendly to advise you either to take the risk of a return journey, because the outcome will depend on your own inner strength. You must look within yourself for the answer.

"But one piece of advice I will offer. If, after you have given it much thought, you decide to make the attempt, I urge you to borrow as many books from your doctor friend as he is willing to lend you and apply yourself seriously to studying."

The day after her visitor left, Harriet stopped in at Dr. Hamilton's consulting room to tell him what she planned and to ask if he would advise her on a course of study and lend her the books required. He was not averse to doing what she asked. "But it's only fair to tell you that your chances of getting a medical degree aren't worth a trip to Portland, much less a three-thousand-mile wild goose chase. You'd be crazy to throw away all the time and effort you've put into your business.

"I don't doubt you've got what they call 'the healing touch.' Many women have it. And it won't hurt to learn what you can from the books. But you'd better be satisfied with lending a hand where and when you're needed, instead of beating your head your head bloody trying to break down a stone wall."

But Harriet was still under the spell of Miss Anthony's eloquence. So she accepted Dr. Hamilton's help, ignored his advice, and decided not to seek any more opinions on her plan. Most likely some, if not all, of her family, would react as he had and she had enough to do to get ready without wasting her energy resisting opposition.

She had assumed that Dr. Hamilton would keep her confidence, but he did not consider theirs a patient-doctor relationship and had no compunction about sharing his opinion with interested parties. One day not long after the conversation, her sister Ellen came storming into the shop to ask if it was true that she had taken leave of her senses.

What followed was the opening skirmish of a battle that lasted until the day Harriet shut her shop. Everyone in the Ferry family was outraged by her "crackbrained scheme." Her brothers were not as voluble as her sisters, but they made their disapproval equally clear, Lyman especially. He had just been appointed to the governing board of the state's Temperance Society and was highly sensitive about anything that might reflect discredit to his organization. When Harriet demanded to know how her ambition to join an honorable profession could do any such thing, he mumbled something about people's willingness to swallow the slander that all advocates of temperance were eccentric or unbalanced.

"You think I'm going to make a fool of myself because I'm bound to fail! I think I'm going to make fools of all of you who doubt me. Time will tell which of us is in the right."

Lyman had nothing more to say. But Ellen's objections came thicker and faster. Some of them were so outlandish that Harriet shrugged them off without comment. But one landed close to the scar of an old wound and started a quarrel between them.

"Of all the times for you to start acting crazy," Ellen said one day. "Just when people were beginning to forget about how you disgraced yourself, getting a divorce."

"There's nothing disgraceful about getting divorced."

"Not if your husband committed adultery. But you never said Will did."

"There are worse things than adultery."

"That's your opinion! People said you were putting it above the Scriptures. Will's mother said you were too irresponsible to be trusted with a child and the proof was that you left Papa's house and took Robbie with you because you couldn't stand to be ruled by anyone but yourself."

"You know the reason I left."

(But maybe she didn't. Maybe Ellen was too young to know about Papa's drinking. Lyman wasn't. His devotion to the Temperance Society was proof of how deeply it affected him. But the family never talked of it, even now that Papa was gone. Perhaps the younger children had been spared the shame. Or perhaps Ellen had managed to forget what she didn't want to remember.)

"Why do you have to stir everybody up again? Why can't you be satisfied with what you have," she was asking now.

"Because I don't want to spend the rest of my life keeping a shop!"

Ellen's face flushed as if it had been slapped. Harriet had forgotten for the moment that Isaac kept a shop, but she was too angry to apologize.

The sisters hardly spoke for several weeks, but Ellen's campaign was carried on by other members of the family. As the day of Harriet's departure approached, even her mother was pleading with her "not to disgrace yourself again." Robbie informed her that he intended to study to be a doctor and didn't think they needed two in the family.

The only person who did not discourage her was Aaron. He asked her for the second time to marry him, but not as an alternative to her pursuit of a medical degree. He was willing to wait for her "triumphal return," or, if she would postpone her trip until he could make certain arrangements, to accompany her to Philadelphia, set them up in living quarters, and busy himself with affairs connected to his business until she had achieved her purpose and was ready to come home.

"I promised myself never to marry again until and unless I was as independent as any man."

"You have been that for some time now."

"Financially, yes, but not in the work I feel destined to do. Now for the first time, I know what that is."

Aaron took this as an indication that she was no longer refusing, only postponing her answer. He did everything he could to be of help: advised her on the choice of transport and itinerary, even wrote to friends in Philadelphia who might be willing to accept her as a boarder. And when at last, she boarded the stage that was to take her on the first leg of her journey, Aaron was the only one to see her off.

It was a miserable stormy night. Harriet was the only inside passenger. She braced herself against the jolting and tried to sleep. When she closed her eyes, she saw Aaron's face. He had wished her every success, but said nothing more. If he had renewed his offer, she might have given him a different answer. The ordeal of these last few weeks had taught her the true worth of fidelity like his. But the lesson had come too late. It would be months, perhaps years, before she could tell him so....

There was no longer any reason to keep up her false front of fortitude and she was sliding into a sea of self-pity. Never had she felt so alone, so vulnerable, so utterly bereft.

※

She had been cold for a long time. What made her aware of it was the pain starting in her knees. Her hands were still warm because she had tucked them into her armpits, but the cold had seeped through the leather soles of her boots and up her legs. They were so stiff she had to grab one of the scrub pines to pull herself to her feet and hold tight to it while she stamped some feeling back into them.

Something was stirring under the surface of her memory, but she had lost patience with this fishing in the past. It had gained her nothing that addressed the decision she faced in the present: whether to end her marriage or accept the lie on which it now rested.

Still too stiff to mount Pride, she led him along the beach till they came on a drift log she could use as a step. Once mounted, she drew healing warmth from the horse's body, and the pain in her knees began to quiet. The ebbing tide had exposed a highway of hard sand. She loosened the reins and tapped her heels against Pride's flanks. He broke into a gallop. Harriet gulped at the wind till it filled her lungs and cleared her mind. On and on they raced, as if to outdistance a pursuing enemy, up to the place where the rock jetty protruded out to protect the bar.

When they turned and started south, she was blinded by the glitter of the sun on the waves. No longer able to make out the line between the sand and the water, she closed her eyes and let the horse find his own way.

Perhaps that was the way out of the morass in which her marriage was mired. Close her eyes to what she could not bear to see. Loose the reins. Let life take whatever course it chose.

That evening, she wrote to her sister Ellen:

"This month I officiated at the birth of a boy whose mother gave him to me. I took the little orphan to my heart and gave him a share of a mother's love. With my husband's consent, I have called him James Franklin IV."

VII.

The ménage at the farm settled into a routine that differed in no obvious way from the old. Millie gradually resumed her old chores about the house and barn. James continued to spend much of his time on affairs connected with the railroad. (When he was home, he was punctiliously polite to Millie and affectionate to Harriet, but hardly seemed to notice the child to whom he had given his name.) Harriet took over the mothering of the little boy, continued to oversee the hired hands who worked the farm, and kept up an active medical practice.

But the heart of the household had stopped beating. What passed for life was a ghostly simulation—a waking dream in which phantoms performed familiar tasks from which all meaning and all feeling had been drained. All in echoing silence, so that she sometimes wondered if her senses of sight and hearing were going dead.

When she made her decision—not to make a decision—she did not foresee the decisions that would follow in its train. For example, if she was not to question the premise on which her marriage rested, she must stop seeking other possible explanations of the event that had shaken its foundation. She must resist the temptation to keep watch on the other actors in this drama, to puzzle out the significance of words or looks that passed between them. Hardest of all for one of her temperament, she must learn to live with sustained uncertainty.

The only way to do that was to keep busy, deliberately to push the limits of what her aging body would bear. Although she no longer discouraged patients from coming to her home, she let it be known that she preferred going to theirs, with the result that she soon found herself answering calls at all hours and in all weathers, under conditions an urban physician would have found impossible. When the route to a sickbed led over a trail so obstructed with logs and roots or so overhung with tangled undergrowth that a horse could not get through with a rider on his back, she went on foot, forcing her way through bracken and sword fern as high as her head, tripping over blackberry runners that ripped at her clothing as she struggled to her feet. In the rainy season she donned hip boots to wade through the muddy tidelands. In the worst winter storms, boats were sent to fetch her.

One day when a southwesterly was raging, there was a knock at the door. Olaf Bergerson, a dairy farmer who lived a couple of miles up the Lewis and Clark River, had come for the doctor on a "matter of life and death." Olaf's wife had died in childbirth some time ago. His mother had been keeping house for him and the children ever since. The youngest, little Daisy, was everyone's favorite, partly because she so strongly resembled the mother for whom she was named. Now she was ill with "the quinsy," feverish, in great pain, hardly able to breathe.

The roads were impassable, so Olaf had rowed the three miles from his landing to the Franklins' and proposed to go back the same way. Coming, he had the storm at his back; returning, he would have to row against it.

Although Olaf was a powerful man physically, and a master hand with the oars, James protested that the odds were against making the return journey safely. He urged them to wait a few hours in hopes the wind would die down.

But Olaf was convinced that delay would be fatal. So Harriet got into her foul weather gear, slipped a few tablets into her medical kit, and followed the distracted father into the howling gale.

They had nearly a mile to go on foot before they reached the landing. The regular trail was under water and the alternative led through a wasteland of wire-grass whose long, tough strands tangled around a walker's legs like rope. There were two swollen sloughs to be crossed, one bridged by a fallen log, the other by a narrow, wobbly plank. By the time they reached the landing where the rowboat was tied, Harriet's boots were full of water and the cold was making her arthritis kick up.

While she settled herself in the bow section, Olaf began peeling off his upper garments. "I ask your pardon, doctor, but if I'm to get you there, I'm going to have to strip near to the skin."

Wind, far from abating, was increasing in velocity. Harriet began to consider alternative destinations. If he could be persuaded to make for the abandoned landing between the Franklins' pier and his own, they would have to make their way across tidelands far worse than those they had already traversed. But it was possible that they would not make shore at all. Every bit of Olaf's strength and skill was required to keep them from capsizing. In this weather that would most likely mean death by drowning, a prospect Harriet did not find altogether unpleasant.

Olaf had been rowing nearly half an hour and he was tiring. She could see the opening of the slough that led to his house, but they were not gaining on it. His arms were pulling less strongly than they had, but if he stopped to rest, the gale would push them back past their starting point. Harriet was considering whether she could move into a position that would let her add her strength to his, when they heard a whistle pitched even higher than the wind. Olaf twisted round in time to see a little steam launch come shooting of the mouth of his slough.

The poor man let out a terrible groan. "She's dead! The baby is dead! We're too late."

But it was not so. The owner of the launch was a neighbor who knew about the Bergersons' trouble. As the storm worsened, he had decided it was more than even Olaf could handle, so he fired up his engine and was steaming to the rescue.

By the time Harriet reached the sickbed, the child had fallen into a restless sleep. The grandmother apologized for having called the doctor out in this weather. "I told Olaf he should wait till the storm blew itself out, but he was half beside himself."

She spoke in a whisper but it was enough to wake the child. She opened her eyes, moaned, and struggled to swallow. Harriet ordered a lamp to be held over the bed while she first coaxed, then forced open the little mouth. Daisy's tongue was furred, her breath foul, the back of her throat fiery red and swollen, and as Harriet had feared a sizeable abscess was forming on one of the affected tonsils. It would have to be lanced.

In her hurry she had neglected to pack her kit of surgical instruments! There was nothing for it but to improvise.

"I shall need a knife," she said. "One with a slender blade and a sharp, thin point. A filleting knife would do well enough." Olaf went so pale that Harriet was afraid he was going to faint but he managed to ask if the one he used to bone out an elk would do.

"Even better, so long as it's sharp. Clean it with sand. Rinse it well. Hold it in the fire till it glows, then plunge it into cold water."

While he was following these orders, she was improvising a brace to hold her patient's jaws apart, wrapping it with clean cotton rags supplied by Mrs. Bergerson, who was holding up better than her son. When all was ready, the oldest of the children was ordered to hold the lamp, while the father on one side and the grandmother on the other pinned down the patient's arms and shoulders.

"All ready? Now!" Harriet pried open Daisy's jaws, inserted the brace, and before the child recovered from her surprise, she had thrust the point of her instrument deep into the swollen mass. As she withdrew, pus followed the knife point. Daisy began to gag. The brace was removed. She was turned over on her side and didn't have to be told to spit out the foul stuff that was clogging her throat.

Half an hour later, she was out of pain, breathing almost normally, and falling asleep.

The Bergersons called it a miracle and thanked the miracle worker in voices breathy with awe.

"The wind's gone down a little, but it's too dark for you to make the trip back tonight," Mrs. Bergerson said. "You look just about done in and he'll get you back first thing in the morning."

Olaf seconded the invitation. "It's not that I mind getting you back, understand. But we need you well, doctor. Can't afford to have you come down sick."

But what Harriet needed was to be alone, to weep for the child she did not save.

※

She had looked on a dream-made flesh—the child through whose life she would relive her own; who would be her constant companion, imbibing the love of her profession with her mother's milk; who would grow up to be the greatest woman physician the world had known. The dream had sustained her through a difficult pregnancy. She was well past the age when most women experience the change. Friends and colleagues warned her that even if she managed to carry a child to term, the chances were it would not be normal. She knew the odds, but she knew that they did not apply to her. The power of her vision would penetrate her womb, would form and protect the life it nourished. It infused her with energy when she tired and anaesthetized pain, overcame fear, conquered doubt. She believed it as she had never believed in anything.

And she was proved right.

The daughter they gave her to hold was perfect. Exquisitely perfect. Healthy and beautiful and made in her image.

Three days of ecstasy. Then the paralyzing blow of loss. No warning. No chance to wrestle with the angel. Simply the word of the attending physician.

She was toppled from the sunlit summit to the darkness of the pit. Then she had James's love to sustain her, to lend her strength in her battle with despair, to support her on the long road to recovery.

Now she was sliding into the same abyss and James was the last person who could help her. She must fight her own battle or succumb. Morning after morning, she woke and lay with her eyes closed, wondering whether it was worth the effort to rise and begin the day's chores. What difference it would make if she failed to perform them? Whether if she lay still and let the darkness deepen around her, she would find peace.

She was still going through what seemed meaningless motions when there was a letter from Ellen, inviting—ordering—her to come for a visit.

"Do not refuse! I have a need that only you can meet."

The need, it turned out, was not Ellen's, but her own. James had written her that his "dear wife was not herself. Her spirits are so depressed that I fear for her health unless a way can be found to help her." Ellen assumed, as James had, that Harriet would confide in her.

"Sisters are closer in some ways than husbands and wives. You and I have told each other things we'd never tell another living soul. And you know as well as I do, Hattie, there's nothing like talking to take a load off your heart."

It was true. As she began describing the Bergerson child's ordeal, Harriet felt a lightening in her breast and a tightening of muscles around her eyes that warned of rising tears. By the time she could make herself speak of the old grief it revived, she was weeping. Not just for the loss of her dream daughter, but for all the losses she had suffered since.

Ellen put her arms around her and held her till the sobbing began to subside. The only question she asked was whether her sister needed another handkerchief. Harriet nodded and Ellen supplied one.

Eventually the pauses between sobs were long enough for Harriet to blurt out a few words. "If I'd been able…if I'd had anyone…but I couldn't talk to…"

"Of course you couldn't. Men don't understand. But you should have written me. I would have come." Ellen bustled away and came back with a cool, damp cloth. While Harriet was using it to wipe her hot cheeks, Ellen asked if there was anything else that needed to be talked out. "We don't have a chance like this often and we ought to make all the use of it we can."

Harriet took a moment to consider. If Ellen had inquired after little James—or James, himself—or even Millie—she might have lifted the lid of Pandora's box. (Was it odd that Ellen had omitted this ritual of greetings after long absence?) Instead, she wiped her eyes one last time, put on a cheerful face and said—and meant it—that she felt a great deal better already.

"Good! Because I have something to propose. I was afraid to mention it before for fear you wouldn't be in the mood." Ellen paused to give Harriet a last chance to beg off, and then forged ahead. "Isaac and I want to arrange an affair—a dinner party or a reception—whichever suits you better. I've made a list of as many of your old friends as I can remember, but you must look it over to see if I've missed any. Not everyone I've put down may still be here in Portland, but I'm sure there are enough to make up as big a crowd as the house can handle." She chattered on about the guest list, the decorations and refreshments, and whether to write the invitations or have them done at the stationers until Harriet interrupted to say she had brought nothing she could wear to such an occasion.

"You can borrow something of mine. You won't believe that wardrobe I've acquired! Aaron has been sending us sketches and patterns from the *Young Ladies Journal*. Isaac stocks the fabrics and trims and accessories, and we have a list of recommended dressmakers for ladies who don't do their own sewing. One of them—the one I've been using—can copy a Worth gown so you can't tell it from the original. Come upstairs and see for yourself." She was already leading the way to her bedroom.

Following her through the open door, Harriet was momentarily blinded by sun streaming in through the two high windows at the far end of the chamber. When her eyes adjusted, she was startled to see someone standing between the windows, staring at her.

A woman, ill-groomed and dowdy, her features coarsened by exposure, drab skirt splashed with mud at the hem. She took a step forward and the image in the pier glass did the same. Both mouths opened and gaped in recognition.

"Why didn't you tell me?" she whispered.

Ellen either failed to hear or chose to ignore the question. She was searching the section of her capacious armoire that was devoted to evening wear. "You've always said blue was your best color and I have two new blue costumes. One of them is high-necked so you could wear it when we pay afternoon calls and it would do for most evening parties. It's patterned silk, powder blue with burgundy trim. The other one's more elaborate but it's even more flattering. Here!" She pulled from its hanger an stunning creation—a bright blue polonaise over an underskirt of ivory lace. "So! What do you think?"

"It's exquisite. But I can't believe it will fit me."

Ellen was sure it would. "We've always worn the same size. I've put on a pound or so since we last compared waist lines, but so have you. Try it on!"

The next time Harriet faced the woman in the pier glass she was holding her breath while Ellen struggled with the fastenings of the short jacket. Her hair had been brushed and gathered into a chignon (augmented by one of Ellen's switches) that was pinned high on the back of her head. It made a considerable improvement in her appearance, but her face was redder than ever from straining to make her waist smaller.

"I won't be able to breathe, Ellen."

"Yes, you will. And you may as well get used to the feeling. All the new designs are for what they call the hour-glass figure. Look. I'll just hold it together for now. If you like it, we can let it out at the waist. But you must try the powder blue before you decide. That one might have to be let out a little more, but it wouldn't be any more trouble to do."

In the end, Harriet chose the afternoon dress. (The elegant polonaise was too intimidating.) They decided to open the side seams and insert pieces stolen from the deep hem, hiding the alterations under the wide burgundy sash. As they sat together, picking at the stitching, they exchanged bits of family news and gossip.

Ellen had just heard from Mama that Lyman was elected president of the state's Temperance Society. He was thinking of moving to Portland where the Society's main office was located. Mama would come with him if he did because he would need someone to keep house. (Lyman had been jilted by his first love and never married.) Harriet reported on the last letter she had from her son. Rob was moving his family from Walla Walla to Yakima where he had bought a larger and more lucrative practice. Ellen finally remembered to ask after the family at the farm. Harriet said everyone was fine. And James's railroad business? Harriet managed a vaguely optimistic answer and volunteered more news of Rob. His wife was expecting again. Rogie had learned to love his baby brother and was looking forward to a sister. Rob said they would name the baby Harriet if it was indeed a girl.

When they had run out of news, they sat silent for a few minutes before Harriet got up the nerve to ask a question that had been nagging at her since Ellen mentioned Aaron's name.

"You said Aaron sends you sketches. From where?"

"From New York! You knew he moved back there, didn't you?"

Harriet shook her head.

Ellen was shocked. "I took it for granted that you and he…but I should have realized! That's why he asks to be remembered to you when he writes to Isaac."

Harriet could think of nothing to say.

Ellen covered the awkward moment with an account of how Aaron had set himself up in business and how well he was doing and how much Isaac appreciated the favors he was able to do for him. She glanced once or twice in Harriet's direction as if expecting some comment or question. When none came, she asked—very casually—"Would you like Isaac to include a word from you the next time he writes Aaron?"

"Yes. Ask him to say…I am well and send…greetings."

Much later, lying in the darkness of Ellen's guest bedroom, she asked herself the question she had read on her sister's face: why had she chosen James over Aaron?

After years of lonely struggle, after having rejected all other suitors—Aaron was the most persistent, but by no means the only one—why had she accepted James without a moment's hesitation? Not because he offered her financial security. She had won that for herself. (As things had turned out, one might have supposed that it was James who married for money. But she knew better. A dreamer he was, but not a schemer. James had never expected to have to borrow from her. When his great venture seemed in jeopardy, he had done so reluctantly, believing she would be richly rewarded by its eventual—but inevitable – success.)

She had found James physically attractive but she had not been swept off her feet by a grand passion. Nor had he. Both of them were well past the age when the heart rules the head. Nor had either of them married in the hope of having offspring. She had supposed she was too old to conceive again and if James had been set on having an heir, he would surely have chosen a younger woman.

The more she thought on it, the less she understood her choice…or his.

The rest of the week of her visit was filled with the sort of social activities for which she had, without realizing it, been starved: meetings with old friends, coworkers in the suffrage movement, and medical colleagues—especially the last. Their shoptalk filled her with wonder and dismay. So many changes had taken place in the practice of medicine since she left the city—new medicines, new devices, new procedures. There wasn't time to have it all explained, but what she heard made her hungry for more and was appalled at how far she had fallen behind in her time away.

On the trip downriver, Harriet dozed and daydreamed, reliving moments of the visit: the brilliance of Ellen's evening party. Ellen, the little sister she had taught how to dress and do her hair, was now a gracious hostess whose guest list affirmed her position in society.… How different the life she and Isaac led from the one to which Harriet was condemned—at least, until and unless James's golden promises were redeemed.

Perhaps when that day came they would build a house in Portland and she would reopen her office there. She would have to work hard to catch up for time lost, but she had faced worse challenges than that and overcome them.

She arrived from Roseburg with a certificate permitting her to prescribe the natural remedies that were the foundation of eclectic medicine and to operate the equipment used for "healing and electrical baths." The medical establishment in Portland was no more broad-minded than Roseburg's. But the contest between the homeopathic and allopathic schools had not been decided, and a large sector of the public was looking for therapeutic alternatives to the "shot-gun prescriptions" of the allopaths. She advertised in *The New Northwest* and got a few responses. The word-of-mouth praise spread by her first patients was good enough to bring a dozen more and they brought others. Before she had used up the money she borrowed from Ellen and Isaac she was doing well enough to rent an office in a good location. In another few months, she began paying off her debt. When Rob turned nineteen, she entered him in medical school.

Two years later, her son had a degree that put hers in the shade. She helped set him up a practice, closed her own, and went back to Philadelphia, determined to enter the prestigious Jefferson Medical College. Years ago, when she studied at the Eclectic School, she and other students had been permitted to attend lectures by Jefferson professors at the Blackley Hospital. In those days women students were frequently egged on the hospital steps. But things would surely be different now.

She began by paying a personal call on the dean of the faculty, told him her history, and asked for admission to the program that led to the degree of Doctor of Medicine. The man listened attentively and declared himself impressed with her achievement and sympathetic with her ambition to continue her education.

"Nothing would please me more than to take you as my student and some of my colleagues would feel as I do. But the Board of Regents would be scandalized at even the suggestion of admitting a woman to Jefferson." There were, however, other equally qualified schools with more liberal admission policies. "The University of Michigan, for example. Their medical school is second to none in America and I believe it has frequently admitted women."

It proved easy enough to gain admission to Michigan's medical school, although catching up with the rest of the first year class was anything but. Harriet had to hire a tutor and burn quantities of midnight oil. It reminded her of her struggle to catch up with the elementary class at Astoria's Academy. She invested the same sort of energy, and the degree she earned was as respected as Jefferson's would have been. And she still had money in her bank account!

By now she was convinced that surgery was "the queen of all the branches of medicine," (a view that would be considered heretical at the Eclectic school), so she decided to pursue a specialist's degree. After a season of unpaid clinical work at Billings Hospital in Chicago, she and two other women embarked on a medical tour of Europe. Female physicians were not only accepted, but honored in many of the Continent's capitals. She was treated with respect by top surgeons, admitted to their operating rooms, and invited to post-operative discussions.

One of the surgeons she most admired invited her to stay on and spend a year or two assisting him. It was a tempting prospect, but such apprenticeships paid only a token salary and her money was finally running out. She booked passage home, arriving in Portland with just two hundred dollars in her pocketbook.

Again luck—and timing—were on her side. The day after she registered at one of Portland's new hotels, a surgeon who was retiring from practice offered her his collection of instruments on credit, to be paid for "when convenient." Later that same day a patient who had read about her in the newspapers begged her to perform an operation that had been discussed in the interview she gave to reporters.

Again she borrowed from Ellen and Isaac, this time to rent a suite of rooms that would serve both as living quarters and offices and tide her over for the months it would take her to establish a practice, quite different from that of a "bath doctor." In a matter of weeks, not months, her little waiting room was so crowded with patients that Harriet needed an assistant. That was when Millie, who had finished the Willamette Medical School course during Harriet's time away, moved in to share her home and her work load.

What followed was the happiest period of her life. She was universally admired and respected, able to use her new status to advance the two causes she espoused: temperance and suffrage. Her consulting and operating rooms were furnished with the most up-to-date equipment. Best of all, she was doing work she loved, tackling problems beyond the competence of most of her male counterparts. She was at the top of the slope.

Now she was at the bottom, practicing frontier medicine, not too different from what her mother and other pioneer women had done. Many of her cases could be handled as well by a midwife or a native medicine woman. When more was demanded, unless time was of the essence, she referred patients to doctors in Portland or Astoria.

When the beetle had reached the bottom of the slope, it shook itself free of the sand and started back up. Why couldn't she? She could open a practice in Astoria tomorrow! Hold office hours two—or even three—days a week. She would be missed at the farm, but they could manage without her if they had to. James could take responsibility for supervising the hands, and Millie could manage the house and the care of little Jamie.

She began to figure the cost and the possible income. With any luck at all she ought to be able to clear all expenses and put something aside. As soon as she had accumulated enough, she would take time off for a refresher course, perhaps at the new hospital in San Francisco her doctor friends had been describing to her. She dozed off and dreamed of revisiting an operating theatre in Vienna, accepting the offer she had been forced to refuse so long ago.

By the time the steamer docked at Astoria's wharf, she had made up her mind. She was going to do it, no matter what arguments James offered against the plan. It was her right and it might be the salvation of their marriage, like the early years when they saw each other so seldom that every moment was precious. She would be again the independent, successful woman he had fallen in love with. It might take some persuading, but he would see that she was right. He would have no choice.

James was waiting at the end of the gangplank with the news that Millie had died in her sleep night before last.

VIII.

The doctor from Astoria who signed the death certificate ascribed Millie's death to "natural causes."

She had been looking what Harriet called "peaked" for some time, but said nothing that hinted at oncoming illness. That evening she put Jamie to bed as usual, cleaned up the supper dishes, put the batter on to rise for the morning's griddle cakes, and retired to her room. When she didn't come down in the morning, James went to rouse her.

"She looked perfectly at peace," he said. "As if she were asleep and having a pleasant dream."

Millie's death upset the precarious emotional balance Harriet had managed to maintain for the past four years. It was based upon anger—righteous and unforgiving—that hardened into a crust over her heart. The shock of loss shattered that crust, leaving a crater-shaped wound. Love—given and received over so many years—welled up like lava. Hot winds swept her first in one direction, then in the opposite. She relived and revised every event of the recent past, every word uttered, every unuttered thought. Questions unasked reverberated in her head and answers that might have spared much pain.

The rock to which she clung while the tempest blew itself quiet was her decision to start up the slope again. It would be harder than she had foreseen, but she had learned to tackle overwhelming obstacles by dividing them into small ones. The one she chose to tackle first—and she expected it to be the most difficult—was obtaining James's consent.

To her surprise, he offered no objection. On the contrary, he pronounced it a "splendid idea" and began making suggestions on how to carry it out.

She would need office space that could be adapted for light-housekeeping, wouldn't she? Unless she would prefer to share an office with another physician and take a roommate in one of Astoria's hotels. In either case, his expertise was at her disposal. Would she like him to begin making inquiries about available space?

Nonplussed by this enthusiasm, Harriet wondered aloud if James realized that she would no longer have time to supervise the workings of the farm. He did indeed. But he had been intending to resume that responsibility now that his time was more his own. Before Harriet had puzzled out the implications of that last phrase, he anticipated her second concern—finding someone to undertake the responsibilities that had been Millie's.

Here again James was determined to be helpful. "There are many young women—daughters of immigrant families, for the most part—who hire out as domestics. Both of my sisters-in-law have Norwegian girls. I'll have them put the word out that we're interested, and we'll see who turns up."

Little as she liked being obligated to any of the Franklins, Harriet had no alternative to suggest. And just as James had promised, within a week two strapping young women presented themselves as candidates for the position. Neither had as yet any command of English, but both carried letters from local sponsors assuring "whoever it may concern" that the bearer was anxious and able to learn. Both seemed intelligent, personable, and willing. Harriet found it so hard to choose between them that she decided—at James's suggestion—to give each a trial period of two or three weeks.

The first seemed to possess all the requisite skills. She gave the house a more thorough cleaning that it was accustomed to, cooked a few simple dishes acceptably well, established immediate rapport with both of the milk cows, and tried to do the same with Jamie, but the boy rejected her advances. James said that was Millie's doing: she had spoiled the child so badly that he would be slow to accept any substitute. But perhaps the second candidate would manage to get around him.

For a while it seemed that she had. For one thing Gudrin's English was slightly but perceptibly better, so she had less difficulty communicating. She ignored Jamie's hostility, treated him in a cheerful, friendly, but casual manner, and waited for him to make the first overture. It took awhile but before the trial period was over, Jamie seemed to have succumbed. In James's opinion the problem was solved.

Harriet wanted to be entirely sure, so she devised one more test. She decided to absent herself for a day and a night, using the time to inspect the office spaces on James's list of possibilities and to spend a trial night in her own first choice among the hotels.

It was late in the afternoon of the second day when she returned to the farm. Before she had her hat and wraps off, Jamie was clutching her around the knees, weeping and babbling hysterically. It took her the whole of the evening to quiet him. She had to feed him his supper as if he was still an infant and rock him to sleep.

James pronounced himself as astonished as she by the tantrum. Nothing had happened during her absence that would account for it. Jamie had accepted Gudrin's ministrations without complaint, though in retrospect it did seem that he had been unusually quiet. James had taken him for a long walk after breakfast. If he had been mistreated, that would have given him a chance to confide. Gudrin's amazed distress seemed entirely genuine. Still it was clear that someone or something had traumatized the child.

Harriet put off her plans and devoted herself to uncovering the guilty party or triggering cause. She exercised all the patience she was capable of without success. Nothing the boy said pointed the finger at either Gudrin or James. But she did gain some insight into the world the child inhabited.

It was a very small one, bounded by the farmhouse and barnyard, peopled by two women and one shadowy figure of man. (James appeared and disappeared at irregular intervals, but played no real part in the boy's life.) Harriet was the dominant nurturing force; Millie, an acceptable short-term surrogate. He could depend on either of the women in the matter of his basic physical needs, but it was Harriet who supplied emotional sustenance. She was, in every respect but one, his mother.

Her trip to Portland was the first time she had been absent longer than a few hours, and the ten days must have seemed an eternity to the child. Then, before she returned, Millie disappeared and James turned him over to the care of strangers. They were neighbors whom Jamie had perhaps seen once or twice before, but he had never been in their home. He had never been anywhere outside the bounds of his home-world. Now he was exiled from it and abandoned utterly.

Harriet's return rescued him from despair but his confidence had been too badly shaken to be rebuilt in a day. Long before he had got used to the first new caretaker, she disappeared, just as Millie had, and another took her place. Then Harriet disappeared again. What if she did not come back this time? Would Gudrin fail him as Millie had? Or was he was doomed to another—perhaps a permanent—abandonment? His hysterical relief at

Harriet's return was a measure of the terror he had suffered. All he could say about it was, "You don't go away, Mama. Not go away." Over and over again.

It was not put as a question, but he expected a response. A promise. One that could not be reconciled with the plan she had made for herself. She was caught in a trap of her own making. When she decided to accept Millie's child as her own, she had assumed the maternal role, played it to the hilt, taking a secret pride in the knowledge that Millie could not contest her hegemony no matter how hard she might try. Now she was hobbled by the results of that victory.

A woman's instinct was to put a child's needs before her own. She had done that when she bore a child before she was little more than a child herself. Then she had been young and strong and full of hope. She was none of those things now. Still, if the child who needed her were her own, she would accept the obligation without a second thought. In the eyes of the law Jamie was not hers. Until she and James went through the legal process of adoption, he was no one's child. But he believed himself hers and loved her as his mother. A love of that sort compelled love in return—at least for a woman it did.

Was it different for a man? She supposed James must feel something for the child to whom he had given his name, but whatever it was did not appear to bind him as it did her. As a girl, she had felt herself "cabined, cribbed, and confined" by the accident of gender, wished herself a boy—and free! As a woman she had broken those constraints and won her freedom, only to lose it again, for a womanly reason.

When she told James she had decided to postpone her return to full-time practice, he seemed more disappointed than she. But he did not dispute her decision. Instead, he began blaming himself for the situation that caused it. He had neglected the boy, but not by choice. As she very well knew, he had been held hostage by a series of crises in his business affairs. But he was now in a position to make amends and he would. She would see. In a matter of weeks—months, at the most—the boy would have outgrown "this childish nonsense." In the meantime they must keep Gudrin on so that they would not have to break in a new girl when Harriet was able to put her plan into effect.

This was not the first time James had implied that he was free—or about to be free—from the burden that had absorbed his time and energy for so long. The two years he had predicted for the working out of his great scheme had stretched into four going on five. Harriet had long since stopped questioning him about its status, partly because she feared to hear the truth, partly because she feared he would not tell it. But now she put the question bluntly: What had happened to the deal?

James confessed—almost, she thought, with relief—that the original one had fallen through. But there were other possibilities, other interested parties with whom he was in correspondence. Sooner or later he would make the right connection. It was impossible not to. Railroads were the arteries that would carry the blood of prosperity to the region. It was only a matter of time before that would be clear to the most stubborn doubter.

Meanwhile they must keep up the payments on their notes. One of the reasons he had been so quick to go along with Harriet's proposal was that the income it could be expected to generate would go a long way toward easing the burden of those payments.

"When do they come due?" she asked. "And will we be able to meet them as things stand now?"

James ducked the question. When she asked again, he became first evasive, then defensive. She persisted and his face flushed with anger. For a moment she saw—or imagined that she saw—a resemblance to Will Ross, flying into a rage because his word was doubted or his judgment challenged.

She asked no more questions after that.

She had no choice but to carry on as before: seeing a few of her patients at the farm, but most of them in their own homes. She went on horseback when possible, otherwise by boat. At the start she took Jamie with her—especially if the call was made in daylight. But it wasn't long before he had grown too active and mischievous. James was doing his best to win the boy's confidence and making some headway. As long as James was at home, Jamie tolerated Harriet's absence without complaint. He was not happy to be left alone with Gudrin, but even on that score there was some improvement.

As winter closed in, everything got harder. Days grew shorter and the weather stormier. Harriet's arthritis worsened. Some days her hands were so stiff that she had difficulty using her instruments. The money her practice brought in barely met their needs. She tried not to wonder how James was dealing with the mortgage payments, concentrating instead on economies in the household budget. The pittance they had been paying Gudrin was one of the first expenses to be cut. Harriet promised that it would be made up to her as soon as she was able to open her office in Astoria.

"And I expect to do that early in the spring."

But before spring came, Gudrin had accepted a proposal of marriage. There was no discussion of hiring a replacement. Harriet assumed the absolutely necessary chores and continued her rounds. But she was asking more of her body than it was able to give. Her knee and hip joints were beginning to protest. She could still mount and dismount from her horse, but if the ride was a long one, it took her several minutes to limber up enough to walk. Her hands were even worse. For days at a time she couldn't trust her fingers to perform simple surgical procedures. She carried on—grimly and glumly—because there was no alternative, either for her or for her patients.

Toward the end of the summer, Rob brought Nora, his new wife, their baby boy, and Rogie for a visit. Glad as she was to see them, Harriet worried lest they ask embarrassing questions about Jamie's parentage. When they didn't, she worried about what that implied. The answer, as she learned on the day they were to leave was that Rob was too concerned about the state of her health to pay attention to anything else.

He took her aside to ask, "Are you trying to kill yourself, Mother? If you were my patient, I would order enforced rest, if possible in a more salubrious climate."

"If I were your patient, you would know better than to order the impossible."

"Why is it impossible?"

She didn't have the energy to explain, and that alarmed Rob even more. If she would not discuss the problem, he would speak to Mr. Franklin about it. Harriet begged him not to. In the end he agreed—on condition that she promise she would do it herself after they left.

She did as she promised—with precisely the results she expected. At first, James refused to accept Rob's assessment. She had never looked better. Everyone said so. Only last week someone had remarked that the doctor had more energy and vigor than most women half her age—something he attributed in part to the pure sea air they breathed, and in part to Harriet's regimen of a cold bath every morning.

He was still talking in this vein when she held up her thick, twisted fingers and showed him the joints that would no longer bend. He gaped at them for a moment, then went into one of his sudden mood reversals.

It was true—he had failed her. But what could he do? Pinch every penny, borrow from friends, beggar himself to keep up the mortgage payments? Also, she must realize that these were unusually difficult times.

"The whole country is suffering. Banks are closing in the East. No one is willing to enter into a new venture, no matter what its potential. But this state of affairs can't last forever. If we can weather this storm—bad as it is—the sun of prosperity will shine on the whole state, nowhere more brilliantly than here in Clatsop County. And you and I will own a sizeable share of that golden future…"

She had stopped listening. She no longer believed what he was saying. It might turn out to be true, but it made no difference. She was condemned to hard labor for an indefinite term.

The six years that followed taught her what it was like to live without hope. She went about her tasks in a state of sullen resentment. Her disposition grew sour, her temper short and ugly. She and James rarely spoke to each other. When they did, it was usually about Jamie. James had made good on his promise to pay more attention to the boy and succeeded in winning him completely.

When she accused him of alienating the child's affection for her, he retorted that she had turned into a person no one could love.

Too burdened to have time for correspondence, she lost touch with friends and family in other parts of the state. Ellen was the only letter writer in the Ferry family, and when Harriet failed to respond, the flow of news was cut off. Cards on Valentine's Day and at Christmas were the only way she had of knowing who was alive and where.

Her relations with the Franklins were colder than ever. She had little or no opportunity to make other friends. She saw no one but her patients and their families, and them only in circumstances that did not lead to friendship.

But her practice gave her something that sustained her: the knowledge that she was filling a real human need, doing it under the most difficult of conditions, and doing it well. She had promised herself—and her patients—that she would never refuse a call. The pride she took in keeping that promise was the most precious thing she still possessed; it made life worth the pain it cost her to live.

It was the worst winter storm in living memory. Fierce winds and heavy rains had begun in late morning. By nightfall, the house was trembling and shaking. By bedtime, the shrieking wind made sleep impossible.

Harriet lay awake and listened, thinking that it would be just her luck to be called out on an emergency. She heard the downstairs clock strike eleven, then twelve, then one. After that she must have dozed for it was almost four in the morning when she was roused by a light flashing across the bedroom wall. Someone with a lantern was approaching the house on foot!

She was already out of bed and struggling into her clothes when she heard the doorbell. James called that he was answering it and she need not disturb herself.

"You're not going out on a call in this storm. I'll tell whoever it is to wait in the kitchen until it abates."

She was dressed and on her way downstairs in another few minutes. The messenger, a youngish man, was drying out by the stove and recounting the horrors of his trip.

"I been six hours getting here, with the wind at my back all the way from Seaside. But there's trees down every few yards. I had to tie my horse a mile or so back and foot it the rest of the way."

"Then you'll understand why I cannot permit my wife—"

Harriet cut off the rest of James's intervention with two curt questions:

"Who is the patient and what is the emergency?"

"It's Mrs. Smith…lives downstream, upstream from us a bit more than a mile. She's having another baby. Some of the neighbor ladies have been helping, but my ma says it's not going right. Didn't say why not."

"How long since the labor started?"

The young man didn't know for sure, but his mother had been in attendance since yesterday evening.

"So it's already more than twenty-four hours. If we can make it back as fast as he came…."

"Harriet, my dear," James protested, "you heard what this fellow was telling me. Trees are falling. Water is rising."

"I have promised to go when I'm called."

"But not to do the impossible."

"There is no other doctor nearer than Astoria. It would take a day to get a message there and another for the return journey." To the young man, "Do you think we can lead my horse to where yours is tied up?"

"It'll take some cutting. But if I can borrow an axe—"

"Find him an axe, James, and saddle my horse. I'll be down to the barn by the time you're ready."

The wind threatened to blow her off her feet several times on her way to the barn. But she reached it at last, climbed on to the new gelding (Pride had gone to his rest the year before), put her head through a hole she had cut in an old blanket, and directed the two men to make its corners, sides, and ends fast to the saddle and cinch—an old Clatsop Indian trick that would not only keep her wraps in place, but also prevent her being blown off by one of the heavy gusts.

James had found two axes and a pair of storm lanterns. He and the messenger preceded her through the woods. Five downed trees blocked their path, and it took two hours of hard work to get around and past them. They found the messenger's horse where he had left it. Harriet's horse followed it obediently, but once they were out of the woods and exposed to the full force of the storm, it opted to follow James back to the safety of the barn. Strait-jacketed by her blanket, Harriet had little or no control, so the messenger had to dismount and lead both horses into the blast, mile after terrible mile.

The sky was beginning to lighten by the time the wind let up. By full daylight, it was quiet and the rising sun was shining under a thin cover of cloud. But their way was still blocked by fallen trees. It was almost noon when they reached their destination.

A tall, haggard man who had been pacing the yard came forward to help the doctor down.

"Are you the father?" she asked.

He nodded. Then, staring at her intently, "Ain't you Hattie Ferry that was?"

"Yes."

"Well, I'll be." He shook his head as if in amazement, but before he could frame another question—or comment—a women emerged from the house and beckoned the doctor to come quickly.

"I don't know but it's too late for the little one," she said. "We couldn't get a hold on him to pull, and poor Miz Smith's too wore out to push."

"But she—the mother—she's still…?"

"She's breathing," the woman said and shrugged.

It was a breech presentation, as awkward as any Harriet had ever seen. The little body was wedged fast in the birth canal. It took her nearly half an hour to free it.

The umbilical cord was wrapped around the infant's neck and had strangled him hours ago.

The mother opened her eyes and her lips formed a soundless question.

Harriet shook her head. The woman's eyes closed.

IX.

The husband had been standing in the doorway. Now he approached, asked permission with a gesture, and took his wife's hand. She did not open her eyes.

"Will she be spared to us?" he asked after a time.

"I expect so," Harriet said.

She had clamped and severed the cord and was waiting for the afterbirth to emerge, hoping there would be no complications. She felt the uterine fundus through the abdomen wall. If there was even the slightest contraction, she could augment it by pressure. But the womb, like the woman, was exhausted and inert. In her medical bag was an ergot preparation that would stimulate contractions, but Harriet was not sure her patient could tolerate ergot's side effects. Better to let her rest, gather strength, then perhaps a very small dosage.

"You don't remember me, then?" the husband said. "Jefferson Smith. Jeffy, I was called in those days." And when she failed to react to either name, "We was in the primary class together. At the Academy in Astoria."

Harriet searched her memory for a face that would resemble his in the class of children with whom she had been forced to recite thirty, nearly thirty-five years ago.

"Of course there was a lot of us," Smith was saying, "and only the one of you."

She was twenty-two years old. The next oldest member of the primary class was eleven. Some were as young as eight or nine. They stared at her as if she were some sort of freak.

When she had told her brother-in-law she intended to apply for entrance to the Academy in Astoria, he begged her to stay with them for the summer. She would have free board and lodging for herself and Robbie in return for helping with chores. If she needed money for her school fees, she could set up a small summer school on the Plains. Most families there had no way to get their children to school in the bad weather of winter, so there were many who hadn't yet finished the primary grade.

Frank lent her his horse and she canvassed the area and managed to recruit sixteen pupils. Some of them were more advanced than she in some of the subjects, but she took the books home at night and, with help from Sister and Frank, prepared the next day's lesson. No one ever found her out.

By the end of the summer, between what her school netted and what she earned picking blackberries, she had enough to pay her fees for the year, with some left over to live on while she looked for work in Astoria.

She found both work and a place to live in an old house on Astoria's waterfront. It had been divided into apartments, only a few of which were occupied. Harriet arranged to pay part of her rent by cleaning, washing, and ironing for the owners and to be paid in cash for doing the washing of two of the tenant families. One of these ladies was willing to watch Robbie during the hours Harriet would be at school—if she could persuade Mr. Deardorff, the principal, to accept her as a pupil.

That was not easy to do. The Academy's pupils were for the most part the young sons and daughters of Astoria's "respectables." Harriet was neither young nor—by Mr. Deardorff's standards—respectable. But she was persistent and persuasive and eventually won the support of his wife, the assistant principal. In the end, the man decided it could do no harm to give her the chance she had worked so hard to earn.

What she had not foreseen—or could have prepared for if she had—was the examination required of every entering student. She did passably well in reading and penmanship, but failed in spelling and in mental arithmetic. She was called into Mr. Deardorff's office and informed—not unkindly—that she would be placed in the primary class until she could demonstrate the expected degree of competence in those subjects.

She went straight from the principal's office to the classroom where the arithmetic lesson was in progress. Places had already been assigned but the teacher interrupted the recitations to make an opening for her. "Mrs. Ferry, is it? Let's see. That would put you between Elliott and Franklin."

Did she imagine it, or did the title "Mrs." start whisperings and giggling in the rows behind her? The girl who had to move one place to the right gave her a cold, disapproving look.

(A girl whose last name was Franklin! One of James's sisters? She might have gone home and talked at the supper table that night about the married woman in the beginner's class.)

And there was worse to come. Called on to stand and recite, she felt like a scarecrow, shabbily dressed in hand-me-downs that had survived innumerable washings. All the other girls' frocks were brand, spanking new, bought or made by their mothers for this auspicious occasion. She stammered out an answer to the teacher's question. It was wrong! The correct one was given by the smug smiling girl who sat next to her. And that was only the first of the humiliations of that interminable day.

As she left the schoolyard that afternoon she was thinking of ways to persuade the Deardorffs to return her fees. Not that she was giving up on getting an education. She would find some other way. Move to another town. Even back to Roseburg...but before she had gone a block, she heard herself called by name.

It was Mrs. Deardorff, hurrying to catch up with her. "Mrs. Ferry. May I call you Harriet? Do you think you could arrange to stay an hour after school on Wednesdays and Fridays? I would be glad to help you catch up for your late start. A bright young woman like you should be ready for the advanced class in no time at all, if you apply yourself. "

Applying herself was what Harriet did best. Bright she was not, if by that one meant quick to absorb knowledge. She had struggled hard for every bit she acquired. She was more than willing to struggle now.

So began a regime that would have daunted anyone less determined. Sunday nights, after she finished the Osens' laundry, she and Robbie bedded down in the Olsens' kitchen. At four the next morning she was up and starting the ironing. Robbie and the Olsen children went to school at eight thirty, Harriet followed them at ten o'clock. On Monday nights and Tuesday mornings she did the same for a doctor's family. On Saturdays she did her own washing, ironing, and mending. The house was built partly on pilings driven into the river, so she and Robbie were able to collect enough driftwood to warm their apartment by scavenging whenever the tide was low. What time was left of each day (and part of each night) was divided between sleep and schoolwork.

As Mrs. Deardorff had predicted, it was only a matter of weeks before Harriet was promoted to the intermediate class. By the time the term ended, she had entered the advanced classes in everything but spelling. (With that she was to have a problem all the rest of her life.) The principal was even sending some of the younger students to her for tutoring.

On the last day of classes, he called her in to tell her she had a gift for teaching. If she pursued her studies with the same good results for the next few years, she could look forward to employment in the county's school system. Meanwhile, what she earned from her tutoring would pay her tuition. All she would have to make up was whatever it would cost her and her young son to live.

Again she taught a three-month school on the Plains and picked berries. She also learned how to mend tears in the crocheted nets used for salmon fishing. At the start of the fall term, she went back to Astoria, rested and reinvigorated, to begin the same arduous regime. But the effects of the summer's rest were not lasting. By Christmas, she had lost all the gains of her "vacation" and fallen victim to a cold that threatened to turn into pneumonia.

Some of her employers considered her almost a member of their family and they were concerned for her health. One advised her to give up working for the rest of the year and devote herself to her studies: "I'll advance you the money you need and you can work the debt off in the summer." Another suggested the opposite: give up schooling until she had earned and saved enough to pay for a year of uninterrupted study. Harriet appreciated their interest, but for one reason or another, she rejected all their suggestions. Then came one she had a hard time rejecting.

One rainy evening in February, she had tucked Robbie into bed and was busy doing her week's ironing and studying at the same time. There was a knock at her parlor door and she opened it to Captain Worthy, a middle-aged gentleman who was a cousin of her landlord's.

Harriet helped him off with his overcoat, offered him her one comfortable chair, and picked up her smoothing iron to resume her task.

"Perhaps I've come at a bad time," he said. "If you haven't time to talk—"

"I can talk and work at the same time. I've trained my hands so they need almost no attention from my brain."

But the captain insisted that she put her work aside.

"I want you to listen well to what I have to say. I have more money than I need and no family to leave it to. Let me pay your school fees and whatever it costs you and the boy to live, for however long it takes you to get on your feet. I know you're determined not to be under obligation to anyone, so you can consider it a loan if you like. Pay it back when you can, or forget it. All

I want is to know you're not ruining your health living like a church mouse, working like an ox, and studying like a monk."

"I do thank you, but I couldn't take money from you."

"Why not?"

She cast about for words without implying that she suspected his intentions.

"You're worried about folks talking," he said. "Well, some would if they was to know. So don't tell 'em. I won't. Not a word to any living soul."

"But people will wonder how I'm able—all of a sudden—"

"Let 'em! Or tell 'em something to shut 'em up. Say an uncle in California remembered you in his will."

She was tempted, terribly tempted. Never to have to lean over another washtub or heat another smoothing iron or push another broom. To have time to study and time to sleep, money to buy new shoes before their old ones were past repair…

"So, what's your answer?"

"I'm afraid it must be no. Please don't think I'm ungrateful. But you must understand: a woman in my circumstances has to be careful—"

"What's wrong with your circumstances?"

"For one thing, I've been married and divorced."

Captain Worthy shrugged his contempt. "Is that all?"

It was not, but if he knew nothing about the other cloud that hung over her, she was not going to inform him, so she mumbled something about a single, young woman having to be careful about her reputation.

"Your reputation's first rate with people who know you. Those who don't have no call to discuss it. What do you care what such people say? A bunch of ignorant, malicious busybodies!"

The argument went on for awhile. Harriet was tempted almost beyond her power to resist. But resist she did, in the end. Thoroughly disgusted, the captain got up to leave. As she helped him into his coat, he muttered that it would take her a long time to get where she was going if she didn't learn some common sense along the way.

He paused at the door to ask a final question: "Why do you set so much store by the good opinion of people you don't give a tinker's damn for?" He did not receive an answer.

More than an hour had passed. The room had grown chilly. Harriet asked for a shawl.

The woman who brought it asked if she wanted the draft opened on the wood stove. "It seems plenty warm in here to me. But you got your damp clothes on still. Would you like me to hunt you up some dry? Miz Smith's near about your size."

The effort required to change from the skin out was more than Harriet felt up to. She was coming down with something. The sooner she got home and into bed the better.

There was still no sign of the afterbirth, but her patient was awake now.

"I'm going to give you some medicine," Harriet said. "It may cause you discomfort, but only for a short while." She rummaged in her kit for the bottle of ergot tablets, shook out two, filled a glass with water, and asked Smith to raise his wife so she could get the draught down.

A few minutes later the woman groaned and pressed her hand to her swollen abdomen. The contractions were starting. Harriet waited in readiness.

At first, nothing came but a little blood. Then, a sudden, strong spasm shook the woman's whole body. She cried out in pain and expelled what appeared to be a section of the placenta and few shreds of fetal tissue. But that was all.

It was the first time she had seen a case of placenta acreta, but she knew what it meant. Most of the afterbirth was still clinging to the wall of the uterus. There would be no more contractions unless it was detached—a delicate and dangerous procedure under the best of circumstances. These were the worst.

Harriet thrust her hand deep into the birth canal and groped with stiff, swollen fingers for the dilated cervix, hoping that the nexus of vessels would be close enough to its opening so she could gently disengage it. When that hope failed, she could think of nothing to do but to pull—ever so gently—on the remaining portion of the umbilical cord.

It resisted. She pulled a little harder. It still resisted. The third time it went loose in her hand almost before she had pulled. The fetal vessels tore away from those that had fed them. A torrent of blood washed everything before it. A massive hemorrhage that she was helpless to control.

By the time she was ready to start home, the sun was low on the western horizon. The young man who had brought her had been sent on some other errand. There was no one to escort her but the bereaved husband and she could not endure the prospect of another two hours in his company.

She assured him she could manage on her own. The weather had turned mild. Light would linger in the evening sky. By now the trail would be cleared of most of the fallen trees and her horse could find his way around any that remained. "He knows the way better than I do."

Smith saddled her horse, led him from the barn, and helped her to mount. "Can you wait for what we owe you?" he asked.

She was about to say that he owed her nothing, but it occurred to her that he might take offense at being offered charity.

"No hurry. Whenever it's convenient," she said and started away.

By the time she was halfway home, she realized that she was feverish. The horse seemed to move with dreamlike slowness while her mind raced faster and faster, back over every moment of the day: every action she had taken or decided not to take, every alternative she had considered, and some she had not thought of till now. What would have happened if she had not intervened? If she had waited longer, another hour or two or three? If her fingertips had not been so numb? What if she had refused the call as James had wanted her to? The messenger would have continued on, crossed the bay to summon another—younger—physician from Astoria—who would have been too late.

But so was she! She had kept her promise, but it had availed nothing. The life of the mother had slipped through her fumbling fingers.

The prop that had been sustaining her was rotten and was giving way.

X.

The sun beating on her head made it swell to bursting, there was an ominous roaring in her ears, she was tired, so terribly tired, but the call was urgent and she was already late.

She was hurrying as fast as she could, but the road was steep and sandy. Her feet kept slipping, sometimes only a step or two back, sometimes farther.

The beetle was gaining on her because its feet had claws that dug into the sand. Maybe if she went down on all fours, she could make her fingers dig like claws. But leaning over made the roaring louder and the headache worse.

And she was thirsty—parched. Her mouth felt as if it were lined with feathers. There was bound to be water at the top, but she didn't seem to be getting any closer, what with the slipperiness of the sand and the terrible heat of the sun.

James leaned down over the edge, offering her a glass of water and then snatching it back. He was only teasing, and when he saw how badly she wanted it, he leaned farther over to hand it to her. But his boot started an avalanche of sand, burying her along with the beetle.

She shook herself free and started off, but there was no way she could make up for the lost time. She would try to explain, make excuses, but the dead woman wasn't listening. Her husband had taken her hand and was leading her away.

Harriet tried to run after them but the climb and the sun had sapped all her strength. It was all she could do to call a warning. "Stop a moment. Please!"

They stopped and turned to look back at her.

"You must lie perfectly quiet. Give the medicine time to work. If you start to move about, you'll make things worse."

The dead woman shook her head slowly, stubbornly, and Harriet noticed for the first time that it was Millie.

Everything blurred and whirled. She had to grab hold of someone beside her to keep from falling.

"There, there, my dear." The voice was James's. "The doctor says you're to lie quiet. Let the medicine do its work." He was wiping a cloth across her hot, aching forehead. "There's no reason to distress yourself. None at all."

"I couldn't help it! I did the best I knew how! But it was too late."

"It doesn't matter."

She struggled for words to refute him, but the cloth was covering her mouth.

"It would have come out the same in any case. You could have saved yourself the trouble. But we won't discuss it now." He was talking to her as if she were an unruly child. "Go to sleep now. That's my dear girl. Lie quiet and let the medicine help you to sleep."

But instead she was talking to the couple, explaining how she came to make such a terrible mistake. "But it would have come out the same in the end. You would have died. Everyone has to, sooner or later, there's nothing bad about dying…"

Millie stared at her with those great round, blue eyes. "You're dying," she said. "Didn't you know? That's why we have to finish the grave."

Her husband had been digging into the side of a dune and cut into a nest of beetles. They scurried away in all directions. He began beating them with his shovel and called that someone must help. Millie offered Harriet her shovel, but Harriet couldn't lift it. She turned to ask James to do it for her.

"You're not going to be buried there!" he said. "I won't hear of it. There's space in my family's plot. I'll speak to them about letting you have it."

She wanted to forbid him from asking favors of the Franklins, but her mouth was stopped by the cloth, or something else, something hard that was being held against her lips. An arm slid under her shoulders and lifted her.

"Take some water. Just a sip. It'll help you get to sleep."

The pressure on her lips relaxed and she opened her mouth to protest. Water poured in. It tasted odd—slightly sweet—as if syrup had been added to mask something bitter. But she swallowed it gratefully as long as the glass was held to her lips.

There was still a roaring in her ears but she now could hear voices through it, men's voices, too faint for her to make out all the words. She was sure they were talking about her. If she could move close to them, she might be able to hear better. But she seemed to be floating farther and farther away....

"She'll sleep now." That was a voice she knew, but couldn't place. "This time I believe the fever will break."

She stopped trying to resist and let herself float into darkness and quiet....

It was her wedding reception. Ellen's parlor was full of guests. James was there, dressed in the old clothes he wore to work around the place. The man he was talking to was Aaron, who was dressed in morning coat and striped trousers, impeccably but conservatively elegant. The contrast was not lost on the other guests.

One of them—an old gentleman whose name had slipped her mind at the moment—was asking if she was sure she wanted to hitch her wagon to any man's star? "There's still time to enhance your mind, you know. You aren't even dressed."

But she would be in a moment. Her wedding gown was hanging in the little room off the church vestibule where brides readied themselves for the march down the aisle. But before she got herself into it, she wanted to steal a look at the crowd.

It filled the church! Looking down from the choir loft, she could see only the backs of their heads, but as the music started, they turned to face the doors from which the bridal procession would emerge. A sea of faces—some that she recognized, some that she didn't. People from all walks of life, from all the different lives she had led: her brothers and sisters and Mama; doctors from Roseburg, those who had befriended and those who had persecuted her; the milliner who had tried to run her out of town; Lawyer Charlton; Will and his parents; Miss Anthony; Mrs. and Mr. Deardorff from the Academy; families she had washed and ironed for; Captain Worthy, who had offered to pay for her education. (It was he who had just asked whether she was sure she wanted to marry) And Franklins! All the Franklins....

Off to one side, held back by the morning-suited ushers, were members of the jeering mob that had thrown eggs at the woman medical students on the steps of Blackley Hospital. They had come to scoff, but they would bear witness to her triumphal march. Up the flower-strewn aisle, bowing graciously to the right or the left like a queen accepting the homage of her subjects. They would watch as she was handed up the step of the nuptial carriage and driven off, showering mud on the mob that stood thunderstruck with awe and remorse.

But first she must finish dressing. She had some trouble finding the changing room—it was hardly more than a large clothes closet. And when she did, her gown was not in it. She had forgotten to bring it with her! Left it hanging in her bedroom at Ellen's. She would have to run and fetch it. If she hurried, she could be back before anyone realized what had gone wrong.

Ellen's house was no great distance, but the street was steeper than she remembered and unpaved. Her satin wedding slippers were hardly suited to this sort of climbing. Someone at the top of the slope was making the sand slide down on her. She was ready to cry with frustration.

"Why are you trying to keep me from getting there?"

"To keep you from wasting your time," said Captain Worthy. "Can't you see that you're climbing the wrong slope?"

They were back in the old argument, but the scene was dissolving, disintegrating into separate bits that were dissolving at differing speeds...

A chair scraped across the floor. Someone had just come into the room. There was an odor of soap. And something else, something medicinal.

"Mother?"

She opened her eyes and saw Rob bending over her.

"Trying to pull you through," he said as if she asked a question. "You've been very ill."

"How did you..."

"Don't try to talk. We think you've turned the corner, but you've still got a long way to go." He consulted his pocket watch. "It's half an hour before your next dose. I'll stay with you till then. You probably don't remember much of what's been going on. I'll fill in some of the blanks. Those I can't, we'll get to later. But only if you lie quiet and listen. Is that a promise?"

It was easy to promise, but she could hardly summon the strength to nod agreement.

Rob's account was tersely factual. From what James had told him, it appeared that something had gone wrong on the return journey from the Smiths'. It was past midnight when her horse had limped into the farmyard. Harriet looked as if she had been wandering in the brushy marshes, but she was too ill to give any intelligible account. Perhaps on one of the many detours around a fallen spruce, the horse had lost his way and stumbled into a bog.

James had decided to save his questions until morning, carried her upstairs, and put her to bed.

But by morning, she was delirious A doctor was summoned from Astoria. The diagnosis was double lobar pneumonia with a strong possibility of complications, several of which had already developed.

"How…"

"Mr. Franklin sent me a telegram."

"How long…"

Rob reminded her of her promise. "For once in your life, you must do the listening, not the talking." He smiled to dull the edge of the irony. "The last time I was here, you may remember, I warned you that something like this would happen if you didn't change your ways. You didn't listen. Mr. Franklin says you don't listen to him either. He says he has tried to persuade you not to answer calls in that kind of weather—"

"I have promised never to refuse a call."

Rob ignored the interruption. "—to see patients only here at the farm."

"He knows very well that's out of the question. Did he tell you why—"

Rob stopped her with a gesture.

"If you mean did we talk about his…financial difficulties? Yes, a little. I'm not sure—" He broke off, frowned, and shook his head. "I don't think this is the time for this sort of discussion. Later, perhaps, when you've had a good sleep."

His evasion confirmed her fears. "We're about to lose everything! That's it, isn't it?"

"If I followed him—and it wasn't easy," Rob continued reluctantly, "if worse comes to worst, you'll be able to keep the house and an acre of ground around it."

She had known it! And not let herself know. After all she had done, all she had done without, to insure against the dreadful prospect of old age spent in poverty. Ruin! When it was no longer possible to start again.

Rob was saying that things might not be as desperate as they seemed. Even if the property was forfeited, James had other prospects. "He's disappointed, naturally, but by no means disheartened. As soon as he can be reassured of your recovery, he intends—"

"I don't want to hear it!" Harriet covered her ears.

"You're quite right. I didn't mean to start on this. Take your medicine."

He mixed and administered a draught of the bittersweet mixture, and promised that they would have another talk before he left for home.

Rob stayed another two days, and on the morning of his departure they had the postponed conversation.

"If you think James is capable of recouping his losses, you are deceived," Harriet told him. "He will never prosper and he will never stop believing that he is about to. Everything we possessed has been sacrificed on the altar of that illusion."

"Not everything," Rob demurred. "You still have your home and the farm."

"Are you sure of that? Besides, even if it is so, we can hardly live on the income from a single acre of land."

"Not even with what your medical practice earns?"

"My practice is finished. Done!"

"Come Mother, surely you don't mean—"

"I shall never see another patient, here or anywhere else."

Rob stared at her as if trying to judge whether she was still delirious. When he spoke, it was in the sort of voice she used with hysterical patients. "I can understand not wanting to go on in this climate or under these conditions. But medicine is your vocation. Do you remember telling me when you came home from Europe, 'Surgery is the queen of medical practice and I am ready to wear her crown.'?"

She remembered, but it only strengthened her resolve.

"You had earned the right to lay claim to a crown and the rewards that went with it."

"I was a different woman then. The one I am now is not fit to hold a scalpel."

"That's your illness speaking. Once you're back on your feet, you'll feel differently. I'd lay odds on it."

"You wouldn't if you knew…" Reluctantly at first, but soon with a sense of relief, Harriet recounted in detail the particulars of the case of placenta acreta: how she had made a supreme effort, only to lose her patient through "incompetent bungling."

"Why do you call it bungling? Under the circumstances—"

"My hands were shaking! Like old Dr. Palmer's, when I took the catheter from him. I am no better than he was."

Rob sat silent for a moment. "I am not an expert on perineal matters, but I've been told that such cases are almost always fatal. Even if you'd had the most modern equipment and plenty of assistance…but you didn't. You've been practicing medicine in places where no other physician will. Providing care to people who would otherwise go without it. If your conscience is too tender to accept a single failure, all the more reason to practice under conditions that alter the odds in your favor."

"Nothing can alter what has happened to my hands."

Rob insisted that some, if not all of her arthritic stiffness, would disappear in a less humid climate. "Take ours for example. Eastern Washington has greater extremes of temperature but the air is drier. People with arthritis notice a difference within a very short time. Besides, the population is growing faster than the supply of physicians. You'd have a practice in no time."

Yakima. To move there would put three or four hundred miles between her and the site of her humiliating failure. Between her and the Franklins, their animus against her and their baleful influence on James. James…

She sighed out the hope his words had kindled. "But James would never consent."

"Then you must come without him."

"Leave my husband? I could never do such a thing."

"You left my father."

They had never spoken of that until now. Harriet had wondered how much her son remembered or had been told. At the time of the divorce, she expected he would hear talk that raised questions in his mind and she had prepared herself to answer. But the questions never came.

Later, when Will Ross turned up and asked to spend a day with the boy, she assumed he would use the opportunity to give his version the facts. She waited for Rob to open the subject, but he never did.

Since then she had lulled herself with the conclusion that Rob's silence meant that he understood and approved the choice she had made. But what if she had been wrong? What if he kept silent all these years because his resentment was too deep to put into words? Perhaps she should have taken it upon herself to raise the subject, explain, plead her case, if not the first time Will made contact with his son, then one—any one—of the other times over the years.

In any case, it was too late now. She tried to read Rob's face, but it told her nothing.

"I did what I had to," she said.

"It should be easier to do what you have to now. You were younger then, but no healthier. You had no education, no skills, no profession, and me to care for, support, and educate. A woman who could overcome odds like that can do anything she sets her mind to."

Relief was pushing tears toward her eyes. She closed them.

XI.

"If you try to resume any of your normal activities before you're fully recovered, you will surely suffer a relapse and recovery from that will take a good deal longer. You're accustomed to thinking of yourself as indestructible. But I hope you've learned what happens when you push yourself past your limits." Rob kissed her good-bye, started away, hesitated and turned back as if he had something more to say, then shook his head and left the bedroom.

Harriet had promised to stay in bed for at least a week. Now she was discovering how difficult it was to change the habits of more than sixty years. Lying perfectly still was like experiencing death. She tried to channel all her vital energy into her mind, forcing it to concentrate on a plan for the future, reviewing all the options available to her, weighing the advantages and disadvantages of each, choosing which she would act upon when her body was ready to support the choice. Her mind did not attack the problem in an orderly fashion. It dodged and darted back and forth in time, replaying the past, rehearsing the future, considering and rejecting one alternative after another.

First to be considered and easiest to reject was that of continuing as they had before her breakdown. If James had not yet squandered the last remnant of their security, it was only a matter of time before he would. What Rob took for courage in the face of adversity was a symptom of his addiction. Sooner or later he would launch another of his ventures, and its failure would doom them to a penurious old age.

Only a miracle could rescue them from ruin, and she must be the miracle worker. But how was she to go about it?

Rob thought she could earn the money to pay off the notes if she went back into practice. It was true that she had once earned considerable sums by performing surgeries that few doctors undertook. But that was a long time ago and she had learned on her last visit to Ellen that there were now a number of specialists in the field of women's medicine. There were probably other venues where she could fill an unmet need, but setting up a new practice would require the investment of some capital. As would buying an existing practice. How much would depend on things she was in no position to assess.

Besides, it might be too late. The properties might already have been forfeited. Rob seemed to assume that they were not. But all he knew was what James had told him, and that might or might not be true. Even if it was—if it was still possible to ransom them—how much money would she have to earn to redeem them? And how much time would she be given in which to earn it? And how could she find out?

Asking questions of James would almost certainly provoke his resistance before she was ready to deal with resistance, and she would not know whether to believe what he told her. But she must have answers before she could make any sort of plan, even whether there was any point in planning, but who beside James could answer her questions? Bankers in Astoria might know who held the notes, but if she consulted any of them, word would get back to James, who could justifiably accuse her of undermining him.

She went round and round this circle of futility until one day toward the end of the week it occurred to her that Isaac Rose had business dealings with several Portland bankers. He would know ways of making discreet inquiries or getting third parties to make them.

She must go up to Portland, tell Isaac and Ellen her problem, and ask for advice and help.

She was ready to get out of bed and dress for the journey, but the physician in her warned that it was too soon. She must rest a little longer and gather strength for what would be a great effort. As she lay there, inert as a corpse, it dawned on her that it had been over a year since she had heard from her sister Ellen, or to be honest, since she had failed to answer Ellen's urgent appeal.

It had come at a time when Harriet was too depressed in spirit to absorb the quantity of sad news it contained: their brother Lyman had resigned his post with the Temperance Society under a cloud. Members of the Board were critical of his handling of the Society's funds. No one had accused him of malfeasance, but he had felt the disgrace keenly. Mama had persuaded him to move back to Roseburg, but it had not helped. He withdrew into a shell like a wounded mollusk and a few months later, he took his own life.

Mama was desolated, crushed, and Ellen wanted Harriet to invite her for a long visit. "Isaac and I would welcome her here, but what she needs is to get away from all reminders of the tragedy. If you and James cannot accommodate her just now, at the very least, you should write her long cheerful letters. She complains of not having heard news of you in ages."

She had put Ellen's letter aside, meaning to answer it and to write Mama as soon as her own depression lifted. She had not done either. Now she would have to explain what prevented her and beg Ellen's forgiveness before asking Isaac for help, and she would have to do it in person, not by letter, as soon as she was fit to make the trip.

Meanwhile she should be considering where to open a practice, if and when she saw her way clear. She ruled out Astoria, not only because its climate was no kinder to arthritis sufferers than Clatsop Plains', but also because of the proximity of James's family. Portland's climate was better, but the competition formidable. Roseburg would present the sort of challenge she would once have welcomed: starting over as a fully qualified physician/surgeon in the place she had once been mocked as a "bath doctor." But that was now out of the question.... If she was to make a fresh start, it had better be in a place where she was not well known, but not a complete stranger either. Yakima would meet both of those criteria. Rob said there was a shortage of physicians, surgeons in particular. The latter was important. The only way she could hope to earn substantial sums of money was by performing the type of operation that had been her specialty in the days when she stood at the top of her profession, when she had sometimes earned more in a single month than she could in a year of country practice.

※

When it was reported that Dr. Ferry had performed the first complete perineal repair by a woman physician, women patients were referred—or found their way to her on their own—in such numbers that she could have restricted her practice to that single procedure. But success in that field opened others and soon she was taking women patients with other problems requiring surgical intervention.

The doctor in Astoria who referred Mrs. Edberg suspected a tumor in the left breast and Harriet's initial examination confirmed the diagnosis. Removal of such a growth was a delicate but not particularly dangerous procedure.

At this stage in her career she often had the assistance of one or two young physicians anxious to learn whatever she could teach them about diseases afflicting women. On this particular morning, however, her assistants were not novices. The anesthetic was to be administered by a professor at Willamette University's Medical School. The assisting physician was a distinguished practitioner of several other types of surgery. Both men expected an interesting, but hardly unique, learning experience.

But the problem was considerably more serious than anticipated: not one, but three tumors. The largest of them was the size of a hen's egg and attached to the axila. To be sure of removing all the cancerous growth, Harriet was forced to remove the entire breast and cut deep into the armpit. A procedure she had never witnessed, much less performed.

When it was over, one of the assisting physicians let out a long breath—as if he had been holding it in suspense.

"Do you realize that you have just done a major operation?"

"You think it should not have been done?"

"On the contrary. It was essential. But if she had been my patient, I would have thought twice before sending her to you. I wouldn't have expected a woman to have the confidence—or the courage—to tackle a job like that."

※

She had neither the confidence nor the courage to tackle the simplest of surgeries now. But as Rob had reminded her, there were clinics for physicians at several teaching hospitals—one in Ann Arbor and one in Chicago. There would be fees and she would need money for travel and living expenses. And since he had suggested a refresher course, Rob might be willing to lend her what it would cost.

And then there was his other, more startling suggestion: that if James could not be persuaded to accompany her, she should leave him behind. That would mean leaving Jamie as well, for the boy was as devoted to James as he had once been to her. After all she had sacrificed for him, all the love she had given when he needed love most! *How sharper than the serpent's tooth it is to have a thankless child.* To be supplanted in his affections by James, who had invested nothing but his...

She reined in her anger just in time. Jamie was as much her child as his—or Millie's—and if he no longer looked to her as his mother it was as much her own fault as his, though that did not make it easier to bear.

Following Rob's advice would have other consequences as well. She would be accused of deserting her child as well as her husband. When she left Will, she had fought to keep Rob with her, but even so she had been vilified. Her reasons for leaving James would be harder to explain—if she were given the chance to explain them, which was unlikely. James's family had the ear of Astoria's establishment. They would poison it against her.

"What do you care for the good opinion of people you don't give a tinker's damn for?" Twenty years ago, she had no answer to the angry old captain's question, but she knew the answer now.

She cared a great deal, enough to sacrifice precious years to secure it. If she had accepted what the captain offered, she could have started her studies years earlier, pursued them longer, been free to expand to the limits of her capacity while she was still a young woman. She had turned down that opportunity in the mistaken hope of winning the respect of people she did not respect. And that was not the only mistake she had made for the same reason.

When she announced to her sister that she had decided to remarry, Ellen embraced her and then—almost as an afterthought—asked who the lucky man was.

"James Franklin, of Astoria."

Ellen had been expecting a different answer and had trouble composing herself. "But you hardly know Mr. Franklin! How long has it been? Two weeks?"

"Three, going on four."

They had met almost by accident. James had come up to Portland on business and was breakfasting with some fellow Astorians. with whom Harriet had an appointment to confer on some matter concerned with the Legislature's upcoming debate on women's suffrage. James invited her to dine that evening, and the next, and the next. He returned to Astoria, but two weeks later he was back. Before that week was over he had asked her to become his wife, and she had accepted without a moment's hesitation.

When Harriet confided that she was for the first time in her life "head over heels in love" Ellen swallowed her disapproval—or was it disappointment—and entered into the wedding plans with generous enthusiasm. Never in all the years since had she questioned her sister's choice, but her silence implied a challenge to it.

Was it the man Harriet was taking as a husband with whom she was infatuated, or the name he was bestowing on her? What illusions she had harbored about the power of that name. The Franklins of Astoria! Even now when she knew them well enough to despise them, she still caught herself sometimes thinking of them as her betters: paragons of respectability, arbiters of the acceptable. As Mrs. James Franklin she would be welcomed into the charmed circle that had been closed to her, all the stigma of divorce, poverty, illiteracy, and menial labor erased.

She had married the wrong man for the wrong reason. Did it follow that....

She stopped short, sat up, swung her feet over the edge of the bed, reached for her wrapper, and got up and moved about the room on bare feet, fighting off the vertigo that threatened by the oldest and most reliable of nostrums—physical activity.

She was well on the way to recovery when she took the steamer to Portland. Ellen and Isaac welcomed her more cordially than she had a right to expect. They accepted her explanation, commiserated over the misfortunes that were her excuse, and left it to her to explain—or not to—why she had chosen this moment to put things right.

It was suppertime before she could bring herself to do that.

"I may as well tell you: we are about to lose everything. There are mortgages on all the property James has invested in, even on what was mine before our marriage. Notes are coming due and we have no means of paying."

She watched their faces as she spoke and saw Ellen's expression change from sympathetic interest to appalled disapproval. Isaac was better at hiding his feelings, but Harriet thought she saw a shadow of apprehension on it and hurried to assure him that she was not asking for anything but advice.

"I have not come begging, Isaac. This is our debt—mine and James's. I mean to honor it, but I need advice on to go about doing it."

Isaac said that would depend on how much was owed. "Can you say—in round numbers?"

"That's one of the things I hope you can help me find out. I plan to go back into practice and earn whatever it amounts to. That is, if they will hold off foreclosing long enough for me to get started. Is there any use asking such a thing, do you think?"

Isaac looked dubious, but said it was not impossible. "Do you know who holds the notes?"

"No, but I'm sure whoever it is is located here in Portland. I have the impression that it's a bank—or possibly more than one."

Ellen's incredulity found voice at last. "How could you not know things like that, Hattie? You must have signed the notes. Didn't you read what you were signing?"

Harriet mumbled that she had been preoccupied or ill or absent when some of the arrangements were made.

But Ellen was not appeased. "It's not like you. After all the times you've lectured me for being careless about money! And what about James? Don't tell me he doesn't know how much he owes to whom?"

Isaac threw his wife a look of reproachful warning and the tirade was cut off.

"James and I haven't talked about finances," Harriet said stiffly. "Not for quite a long time."

"Tell us about your plans to go back into practice." Isaac steered for quieter waters. "I remember that you wrote some time ago about the possibility of opening an office in Astoria."

Harriet explained that Clatsop County was too hard on her health and that she hadn't decided where to go instead. "And I may as well say right now: I haven't confided any of this to James. There'll be time enough to hear his objections when I have arguments to refute them."

Isaac and Ellen exchanged another of the kind of looks that enable well-matched couples to communicate without words.

"You asked if the lender—or lenders—might grant you a moratorium," Isaac said. "Such a thing is not unheard of and in your case the difficulty of liquidating the debt by the sale of the property would be considerable since the property—or the greater part of it—is a hundred miles distant. That is assuming that the lender—or lenders—are in Portland, which we do not know yet."

"But you can find out, Isaac. Just ask your—"

Isaac held up a hand to beg Ellen to let him finish. "If the amount owed is considerable—and we suppose it to be, but we do not know for sure—the sale of the foreclosed property might not realize enough cover it. If the mortgagee could be assured that you are willing and able to pay it off in full, he—or they—would have every reason to grant you some time."

Ellen couldn't keep still any longer. "Anyone who knows or cares to find out how successful Hattie was wouldn't need much reassuring. All you have to do is find out who it is."

"There may be more than one, and that would tend to complicate matters. Some might agree, others might not. Or different lenders might want to impose different conditions."

"Let's cross those bridges when we have to," Ellen said. "The first thing to do is find out who and how many, and of course, how much."

Isaac promised to call on his personal banker in the morning and ask him to make inquiries and to report the results as quickly as possible.

She and Ellen spent another of their "catching-up days," mostly talking about Lyman. His death still haunted them both.

"He just couldn't face the disgrace. It was hard enough on the rest of us. Not so much on me, because being a woman and married I don't have the same name, and most people don't know we were related. That's why I told Mama he'd do better to stay here in Portland and let it all die down. City people have other things to talk about. Every day something new, and pretty soon no one remembers yesterday.

"But Mama thought Roseburg folks might not have heard about it. Or if they did, they wouldn't care all that much. At least, knowing Lyman ever since he was a baby, they'd give him the benefit of the doubt. But taking his own life like that! Well, people began to think maybe he was guilty after all."

Harriet realized that Ellen assumed she knew the basic facts without which it was difficult to follow what she was saying. It would be hard to explain how she had managed to remain ignorant of something that had affected the family so tragically.

"I was ill when you wrote," she said apologetically, "and I never got clear on what the trouble was—something to do with the Temperance Society, I know. But what exactly was he accused of?"

"He wasn't accused! At least, no one came right out and charged him with anything. Of course, as Isaac says, he should have been paying more attention, but he never had a good head for figures. Mama says he was kept back in school once because he failed in mental arithmetic."

"Was there money missing from the treasury?"

"That's what some people think. But Isaac says the accounts were so badly kept that you can't tell how much came in, let alone how much went out and for what. He thinks it was the bookkeeper. The man quit his job and moved away not long before all this came out." She took in enough breath to power a profound sigh. "Poor Lyman! He was so proud of being made president. I wondered at the time why he would want to take on such a big responsibility."

Harriet did not wonder. Ellen was too young to have felt the effect of Papa's shameful secret, but Lyman was not. It would be hard to explain to her—or to any of the younger siblings—what it must have meant to be honored with the highest office of the Temperance Society.

"It's Mama that has it the hardest. She says everyone in Roseburg has a different opinion. Some people think he killed himself so he wouldn't be brought to trial and convicted. Other people—some of her oldest friends—think he was a sacrificial goat lamb for someone higher up, someone who was too important to prosecute. And all sorts or others have even crazier ideas."

"How is Mama bearing up?"

Ellen sighed again and shook her head. "I think she ought to move back here with us. But she says she has nothing to be ashamed of and running away wouldn't help if she did."

Harriet agreed. One would have to run farther than Portland to escape the long shadow of disgrace.

Isaac came home that evening with encouraging news: the sum was "not inconsiderable," but the lenders—two different bankers—were local. Each was privy to the other's claim, and they were agreed on the virtue of a common approach to what threatened to be a substantial loss.

"There is a legal complication that seems to work in your favor: something to do with power of attorney you were assumed to have signed, but which Mr. Franklin has been unable to produce. A clouded title makes foreclosure an even less desirable option. They are assuming that if they come to an understanding with you, the question of the title becomes moot. But they do require a down payment—to seal the bargain and show good faith."

Harriet's bubble of hope deflated. "For the moment, I have no way to pay anything. Can you persuade them to wait until…"

"There's no need for that. I have already informed them that I am willing to advance the sum they require."

Harriet's gratitude was heavily laced with shame.

"I said I hadn't come begging and I meant it. You've bailed me out too many times already. I swore I'd never impose in that way again."

"You have repaid every cent we ever lent you, and I have every confidence you will do so again."

Ellen threw her arms around her husband, and then around her sister, and they all patted tears from their eyes.

It was the first time Harriet had visited her son's home since his second marriage. Rob welcomed her warmly and Rogie's greeting almost knocked her off her feet. Nora reprimanded the boy, kissed Harriet's cheek, and remarked on her miraculous recovery.

"Rob came back from his last visit saying he didn't know whether he'd see you again in this world."

"Come now, Nora! What I said was, I didn't know whether I'd ever see Mother restored to health."

Harriet smiled. "And what you said to me was that I could do anything I set my mind to doing."

"I believed it! I still do. But I thought it would take considerably longer than a month."

She was to share a small bedroom with Rogie, and once her small traveling case was unpacked and Rogie brought up to date on news of the farm and barnyard, she and Rob sat down in his office for a private consultation.

"Do you remember what else you said to me? About opening a practice in a healthier climate and how much better this dry air is for arthritis like mine?"

"You're thinking of locating here?"

She was not sure how to read the tone of Rob's question, and it shook her newly won confidence. "I though you said there was a shortage of physicians here."

"And there is."

"But?"

Rob took so long to answer that she was prepared for the total rejection on any one of a number of grounds she had not considered till now.

"I'm not sure this is the sort of opportunity you're looking for," he said at last. "But it happens there is a practice on the outskirts of town, there for whoever wants it. It belonged to a man who was killed in a hunting accident. The estate has offered it for purchase some time ago, but there were no takers. Most of his patients have found other doctors, but the office is still there. And I believe there's some equipment that wasn't bought in the sale. It would be a start, but not a very auspicious one."

"Did the practice include surgery?"

"Not that I know of. But you'd be starting from scratch in any case. You could build whatever kind of practice you want, and there's no one in the area doing perineal repair or things of that kind."

Harriet asked about the office: was it in reasonably good condition, were there living quarters close by, was there a pharmacy attached?

Rob couldn't give her a firm answer to any of the questions, but he had some house calls to make in that general direction if she wanted to go along, they could drive by the place on their return and she could see for herself.

The office had been constructed in the front half of an old frame house. The original parlor had been converted into a waiting room by the addition of two long benches. A reasonably efficient consulting room had been constructed in the old dining room. The kitchen area had been used as kitchen-dining room-parlor by the bachelor doctor. Upstairs there were four tiny bedrooms, three of which had been used for storage and left to whatever varmints managed to gain entrance.

It was not an inspiring environment, either as an office or a residence. But she had made do with worse. And it could be rented—without repairs—for almost nothing. James could do the absolutely essential renovating. Jamie was old enough to help him. They could bring household furnishings from the farm and she could make new curtains for the parlor.

She was ready to commit herself, but something in Rob's manner mystified and deterred her. After all, it was he who had urged her to this move. Had he changed his mind? Or had it changed for him by Nora, whose greeting had seemed cool? Was she just imagining that Rob no longer wanted her to settle near him? And why couldn't she summon the courage to ask him directly?

At supper that evening, Harriet said she would like to sign a lease on the vacant office. "But before I could begin to practice—here or anywhere else—I must do what you suggested."

"And that was?"

"Go back for a refresher course. As I recall, you said there was one at Billings in Chicago, and another in Ann Arbor."

"That's right. The one at Billings runs for six weeks starting in July and lasts through the first half of August."

So he had made inquiries on her behalf. That gave her the courage to ask, "Did you happen to inquire about the fee?"

"I should have, but I didn't," Rob said. "But whatever it is, I'll be glad to put up, as well as what it'll cost you to get there and back and to live while you're studying." Then, as if he wanted to forestall any thanks, he asked about James's probable reaction to the move.

"He won't be happy about it," Harriet admitted. "But he wouldn't be happy anywhere outside of Clatsop County. Unfortunately at this point, he doesn't have a choice."

The only time Nora had spoken since they sat down to eat was when she felt it necessary to correct Rogie's table manners. Harriet had supposed she wasn't interested enough to listen. But now Nora entered the arena as a defender of James.

"Don't you think it's a lot to ask for a man his age? To give up his home and move to a place he's never even visited?"

"It has been my home as well as his," Harriet said sharply. (More sharply than she should have, as she realized later.) "But if something is not done, it will no longer be ours. We will be paupers, dependent on others for food and shelter."

Harriet went up to bed when Rogie did, read him two stories, tucked him in, kissed him, and put out the light. Rogie went off to sleep at once, but she lay there staring into darkness, reliving the events of the day, projecting herself into the future. When Rob and Nora came up to bed, she could hear their voices through the thin wall between their bedroom and hers.

Rob was answering a question his wife must have put: "If I know Mother, she'll pay back every cent. But even if she didn't, I owe her that and more." He went on to describe his mother's long sacrificial struggle to finance his education, and Harriet's heart swelled. Rob never said such things to her. It was doubly precious to hear them said to someone else, someone who was clearly not disposed to like her.

After a little while, Nora asked, "What sort of a mother was she? In other ways?"

"Demanding. Not so much when I was little, Mother's at her best with very young ones."

Nora asked another question of which Harriet caught only the final words: "…like she spoiled Rogie?"

Rob's answer was inaudible. And the silence that followed gave Harriet time to ponder the implications of Nora's question. Was Rogie's devotion to his G'amma a rebuke to his stepmother? Or was it the prospect of having her mother-in-law as a neighbor that soured Nora? And what, if anything, could she do to win Nora over?

Rob's voice was raised in surprise. "That's an odd sort of question. Why do you ask?"

"Well, she doesn't strike one as being…well-suited to marriage."

Rob began a long account of the difficulties his mother had experienced in her marital ventures, but his voice trailed into silence before he finished. Then—just loud enough for the words to penetrate the wall—he said something that astonished Harriet.

"Maybe you're right, my dear. But being a mother is different from being a wife. Or at least it requires a different set of talents."

When Harriet told James what she proposed to do, he showed a temper she had never seen before. She stood her ground, and the quarrel that ensued was ugly. Terrible things were said on both sides. There was a moment when James threatened to turn violent, but Jamie, who had crept out of bed to eavesdrop, burst into loud wailing. By the time he was quieted, James was sagging like a deflated balloon, ready to ask her forgiveness and accept whatever conditions she imposed.

"You can come with me or stay here, whichever suits you," she said. "But if you decide to come, you must find a good tenant for the place. One who will keep up the farm and do whatever is needed to the house. I shall be in Chicago for sixty days. When I come back, you must be ready to leave for Yakima."

"Why Yakima? It may well be that your practice would be more lucrative in Portland. Or even in Salem. I could accommodate myself to a sojourn in either."

"I considered a number of cities in Oregon before making my decision. Yakima offers advantages none of them can match."

"Have you considered that my future is as much at stake as yours?" James's temper was flaring again. "I must warn you: if I am forced to leave Clatsop at this point in our affairs, we may suffer irremediable loss."

Harriet bit her tongue to contain the obvious retort. After a moment James sagged again, complaining that he had "not a single acquaintance in that area."

"Then you will have to go about making some. You have never been shy with strangers."

"But I shall have nothing to do."

"Find something. With your education you should be able to find work anywhere."

James gave up the battle. In a voice heavy with self-pity, he asked how long he was to "be exiled to this wilderness outpost."

"For as long as it takes me to earn the sum we need to pay off the notes and secure our future."

XII.

She was taking unusual care with her toilette this evening because she had been invited to attend the annual gala supper of the Ladies Reading Club at the home of her friend and patient, Nina Frobisher. Mrs. Frobisher was proposing her for membership in the club and was using this opportunity to introduce her to the officers and members of the board.

Since moving to Yakima, Harriet had managed to pay her debts to Rob and Isaac and keep the mortgage holders satisfied. But the stringent economies she practiced had reduced her wardrobe to the point where it did not hold a single garment appropriate for an occasion like this evening's. She decided to indulge herself in the luxury of a new spring ensemble. (Winter still lingered in Washington, but whatever Harriet chose would have to serve for more than a single season.)

Ellen sent some sketches of Paris fashions for the coming spring, from which, after much consideration, she selected a light wool suit: the skirt cut in the new "bell shape," the jacket, short and double-breasted, and two blouses—a white linen with a pleated bosom and a pink silk with a wide lacy collar. Worn without the jacket, the latter made the costume acceptable for any but the most formal of occasions.

Mrs. Frobisher's dressmaker had studied the sketches and accepted the challenge of converting them into wearable reality, but she warned that the design of the skirt made it imperative to wear one of the new flat-front corsets. The doctor's views on a fashionable figure attained at the expense of the wearer's lung capacity were the subject of controversy in the circles the dressmaker served, so she expected a protest. But Harriet was forced to admit that the skirt she fancied assumed a flatter front profile than her muscles could manage without help.

In other ways, the new styles fit most of her criteria for healthy female apparel. Trains were, thank heaven, passé. Skirts reached only to the wearer's toes. The bell-shape of the skirt could be sustained with a single petticoat, preferably one with a stiff taffeta ruffle. Two years ago she would have protested the long rows of tiny buttons that fastened the long, tight sleeves of the new blouses, but now she could manage them with no difficulty—evidence that the climate had proved as benign as Rob had predicted.

The finished garment surpassed her expectation. The color of the wool—a lighter shade of blue than that shown in the sketch—and the shell pink of the blouse flattered her natural coloring and reminded her of the days when she had been described as "right pretty." But the crowning glory of the outfit was the hat, one of the new pancake straws that Isaac's store would be featuring next month. Harriet had trimmed it with a large silk peony that drooped over the front edge of the brim. A wide grosgrain ribbon, dyed the same shade of pink, encircled the crown and ended in back with a flat bow that balanced the flower.

The woman she saw in her chiffonier mirror looked more like a vigorous forty-year-old than a recovered invalid over sixty.

In the hour before supper was served, Mrs. Frobisher made a point of introducing "our good doctor" to those club members she did not already know. One of the ladies had heard that Dr. Ferry-Franklin was related to that nice young doctor Ross who had moved to Pendleton last summer. "Someone said you're his mother. But how can that be when your names aren't the same?"

It was impossible to satisfy her curiosity without going into details of Harriet's marital history that she still found embarrassing. Luckily, Mrs. Frobisher chose that moment to introduce her guest to the member in charge of the club's educational programs, who wanted to know whether the doctor would be interested in leading a discussion at one of the summer meetings on some topic of general interest.

"I understand that you have published an article on the benefit to women of riding astride, rather than side-saddle."

Harriet acknowledged that she had expressed her strong opinion on the subject in a letter to a newspaper in Oregon. She was willing to present the same arguments to the Reading Club at any time. "But you must understand that for a physician, the needs of one's patients take precedence over all other obligations. If I am called in an emergency, I must go—no matter what commitments must be broken."

"If we're going to ask the doctor to speak, why not let her give the address she made at the Women's Conference in Portland?"

The suggestion came from the only one of Harriet's patients with whom she had discussed her views on the rights—and wrongs—of women, a young widow name Mrs. Marlin who worked at the public library. She was a reader of Mrs. Duniway's feminist newspaper, which had carried a full account of that auspicious gathering, including the part Harriet had played.

"She was up there on the platform with Miss Anthony. And when she got up to make her speech there were two little girls—somebody's daughters, I suppose, but it didn't say who—they presented her with a bouquet of white roses tied with a blue ribbon that matched the one she was wearing across her breast. She must have looked a picture!"

"And what was the subject of your address?"

The question was addressed to Harriet, but Mrs. Marlin answered. "It was about the temperance movement and how it relates to the struggle for women's suffrage."

A venerable old lady seated by the fire had been leaning forward, trying to catch the conversation. Now she asked in what she probably intended as a whisper, "What's that about women suffering?"

Mrs. Frobisher leaned down and spoke into the old lady's good ear. "Mrs. Jackson, I'm sure you've heard of our guest, Dr. Ferry-Franklin, but I believe you have not had the pleasure of meeting her."

Mrs. Jackson peered up at Harriet and smiled uncertainly. "She's a doctor, you say? This little lady?"

"And a very distinguished one. We're told that she holds the honor of being the first woman doctor west of the Rockies."

"You don't tell me!" Mrs. Jackson looked even more uneasy than before. "Well, I hope she's not one of those what-do-you-callums. In favor of women having the vote."

A hush seemed to fall over the parlor as Harriet replied that indeed she was. "I believe there is no power as great as that of the ballot. Women have the right and the duty to use it for the general good."

Mrs. Jackson's tongue clucked several times. "I cannot believe it! Such a sensible looking young woman."

By now all other conversation had ceased. Harriet felt obliged to defend her position and the words that came to her mind were those she had used at the conference. They sounded more radical here than they had in that context—perhaps because Mrs. Jackson had cupped her hand behind her ear and was making an effort to follow, still clucking disapproval and shaking her head.

"Well that's as it may be," she said when Harriet paused for breath. "Of course, I know nothing about this women's movement, but I do know that I am bitterly opposed to it."

As Mrs. Frobisher continued with her introductions, the cordiality of other greetings quieted any apprehension Harriet had felt. She hadn't expected such a confrontation, but neither had she expected so warm a welcome from members of an elite she had assumed to be as smugly conservative as Astoria's. Apparently young Mrs. Marlin was not the only one with enlightened views.

The introductions finished, Nina excused herself for a final check of the table arrangements. Some of the younger women were arguing the pros and cons of spicing up the club's "educationals" with some stimulating, if controversial topics, when a servant came to inform Harriet that she was wanted on the telephone.

The caller, who said his name was Carlson, was in such a high state of anxiety that it was hard to follow his account of the emergency that required her help. Clearly someone was ill—very ill—and the doctor who had been in attendance was for some reason unavailable. Could she come right away? He would hire a carriage to bring her.

"I will drive my own carriage if I come," she said firmly. "But before I agree to do that, I must have a little more information about the patient and the symptoms of the illness."

Carlson's answers convinced her that it was indeed an emergency. She asked for the address and—since it was "a few miles out on the road to Ellensburg"—for direction on finding it. Then she called the livery stable, ordered her horse hitched up and her carriage brought, and went to take leave of her hostess.

"You're not thinking of starting out now? In weather like this! It's been threatening all day and I wouldn't be a bit surprised if we have one of those late snows. I'm sure it is can wait till morning."

"Not if it is a case of diphtheria." Harriet explained briefly but succinctly the nature of disease. "A few years ago it was almost always fatal. The new antitoxin has radically improved the recovery rate, but only if it is administered early. So there is no time to be lost."

Mrs. Frobisher was awed into agreement.

She went first to her office to pick up a vial of antitoxin, a shawl for her knees, and a scarf to wrap around her head in place of the pancake straw. The man who brought her carriage from the livery stable knew the Carlson family.

"If it's on the Ellensburg road, that's young Leif Carlson's. The Carlsons—that's his dad and ma—they live the other way. You sure it wasn't them called you?"

"It was a man. He didn't give his Christian name, but he said the patient was his daughter, and she was visiting her brother when she was taken sick."

"That'll be young Leif. He bought the old Rogers place a couple years back. Did the old man say which daughter was sick? They've got three. My wife went to school with Britta. She's the oldest. Got married last year. Then there's Sally, she's the next, and then Maia. She's not out of her teens yet. Sally's the prettiest. Real nice, too. Everyone thinks a heap of Sally."

By this time he had helped Harriet up, tucked the shawl around her legs, and been assured that she did not require his services as driver. She bade him good night and started off at a brisk pace. His account of the family constellation filled in some of the blanks in the distraught father's account of things:

"It's our middle girl." He hadn't spoken her name, but it must be Sally. *"There's been sickness in the house. Not our house. It's my son's. His wife, she's expecting, so the girls have been going up to help out. One at a time, spelling each other.*

"Then the baby come down sick, so yesterday my wife had me drive her up. When we seen how bad off he was, we got them to call the doctor—their regular one—and he come last night. By then Sally was feeling poorly. He looked at the both of them, give them syrup for sore throats, and said he'd be back this morning to see how they was.

"He never came! We called his place but there wasn't no answer. Maybe he's come down sick himself. And this evening it's worse. She can't swallow at all. Can't hardly breathe even..."

It wasn't clear which of the two patients—the baby or the young aunt—was in crisis. And there were other questions that Harriet wished she'd asked. But there would be time enough for that when she got to the sickbed.

Meanwhile she found herself reliving the pleasures—and the discomforts—of the interrupted evening. It had not gone as smoothly as it might have. But she had no doubt that her application would be accepted.

Admission to membership in the Ladies Reading Club would represent a second—perhaps a conclusive—victory in her struggle to gain a respected place in the community. The first was her recent election to the presidency of the Medical Association. It had been virtually defunct when she took over. Her male colleagues had been more than wiling to let her assume the onerous tasks of collecting the back dues, persuading the lapsed members to rejoin, and convincing the rest to put aside their petty professional rivalries and unite in the best interest of the profession. The effort had cost many letters, many personal calls, and all of her powers of persuasion, but it had been successful. She had been thanked, praised, and elected to a second term—a gratifying contrast to her experience with the medical establishment in Roseburg.

But acceptance by the ladies of Yakima's society had been slower to come. Her friend Mrs. Marlin had confided more than once that the opinions she and the Doctor shared were considered outrageous by some of the older members. Mrs. Jackson was perhaps the oldest, but not the most conservative of them.

What surprised Harriet more than the old lady's disapproval was the number of inquiries about "your charming husband and your little son." (James had complained that he was as isolated in Yakima as a prisoner in solitary confinement, but his confinement had apparently been anything but solitary.) The explanation she was accustomed to giving for their return to Clatsop was that Jamie found the school there more to his liking.

※

Jamie had stubbornly refused to make friends in the neighborhood. They had hoped that he might find at least one congenial soul among his schoolmates, but from the first day on, he had nothing good to say about the teacher, the other students, or the school itself.

One morning he had set his feet like a mule and simply refused to leave the house. All they would drag out of him was that he was being teased. People were saying mean things about his father. Neither she nor James could get him to elaborate. It occurred to Harriet that Rogie might be more informative, so at the first opportunity, she paid a call on Nora and asked if she had heard anything that would throw light on Jamie's problem.

"I've been wondering how long the poor little fellow would have to put up with it," Nora said. "If you want to know what the teasing is about, Rogie was asking us the other day if it's true that his grandpa has to wear an apron when he's at home so you can wear his trousers."

Harriet managed not to flinch. She had been aware for some time that she was failing to win her daughter-in-law's approval—let alone her affection—but not of the intensity of Nora's hostility. Now, as she walked the few blocks between Rob's home and her own, she was remembering the jeering rabble outside the shed in Roseburg and the egg-throwing mob that block the steps of the hospital in Philadelphia. Nora's face appeared in the front ranks of both.

Righteous indignation anaesthetized some of her pain, but as her anger faded, she had to admit that there was some truth to the teasing. James had indeed become a pitiable figure. She was partly to blame, but not for the reason the teasing implied. If wearing an apron meant doing the work of the household, James had never worn one. He was unwilling—perhaps unable—to perform even the simplest housekeeping duties. No amount of nagging persuaded him to pick up after himself or his son. The cleaning of her office and their living quarters fell on her, as did the cooking. She had long since given up baking (which was the kind of cooking she most enjoyed) and worked out a rotation of simple but nutritious meals, the main preparation of which could be done on Sunday evenings and which—with the addition of fresh vegetables in season—could be served through the rest of the week. She also drove her own carriage on her round of house calls. It was a tribute to her recovered health that she could manage it all. James, in contrast, seemed to be suffering from a debilitating disease. He made no friends, found no business connections, no avocation to occupy his days. When the weather was pleasant he sat on the porch, nodded to passersby and arriving patients, and handed Harriet into her carriage when she drove off on her rounds. Sometimes he and Jamie went for walks—two disconsolate figures, proclaiming their misery to whomsoever it concerned and to many it did not. No wonder people pitied him.

She should never have let them come. Or rather, she should not have left it to James to choose whether to come or stay. For a little while Jamie begged so hard not to be "taken away" that James seemed on the point of giving in to him, and she thought she would not have been sorry if he did. The obligation she was undertaking was heavy enough without adding a reluctant husband and an even more reluctant son. She was convinced that Jamie would never be reconciled to the move or forgive her for forcing it upon him. Asked to choose between losing his mother and losing the safe little world of the farm, he would have opted for the farm.

What had happened to the little boy who threw his arms around her and begged her never to leave him, to the love that once bound her so tightly to him? For that matter, what had happened to the love that bound her to

James? While she waited for him to make the decision that might sever both those bonds, she found herself less and less sure that she was prepared to give up on her marriage.

It had not been a bad bargain as such bargains go. With luck, it might have been better than most. If she had not lost the baby; if she had not moved into the range of his family's hostility; if she had played a more active role in the great railroad venture. She should have insisted on being privy to all aspects of it, kept James out of the kinds of trouble his naive optimism exposed him to. He might have succeeded. Perhaps not on the grand scale he dreamed of, but well enough to provide them with a modest living. They might have gone on as they had in their first years together when all either asked from the other was companionship—affectionate, supportive, dependable. Their needs were different in many ways, but this one they shared. And as age cut them off from other people and other pleasures, they would need it even more urgently.

When James finally decided that he "could not bear to be separated from her," she assumed he had been doing the same sort of reassessment, that he too was hoping they could renew their marriage on a more durable basis, using the wisdom they had acquired by its near failure. It was a false assumption that had done violence to her hope.

What he had decided, it seemed to her now, was that he couldn't face up to the tasks of managing the farm, the housekeeping, and the child without her to lean on. He had paid dearly for his cowardice. So had Jamie and so had she. But it might have gone on till it destroyed all three of them if she had not finally been made angry enough to break the impasse.

Mrs. Marlin had dropped in unannounced late one afternoon and found Harriet on her knees scrubbing the kitchen floor.

"The idea of you doing that kind of work, at your age and at the end of a busy week," she exclaimed indignantly. "Why don't you have someone come in to do it for you?"

Harriet could think of no answer that wouldn't reveal the precarious state of the family's finances, so she asked a question of her own—one she regretted the moment it was spoken.

"Why is it that women who do what used to be call 'men's work' are expected to do women's work as well?"

"Because we're fool enough to do it, I expect."

Harriet already knew her friend's sentiments on the question of suffrage, but she was not prepared for a tirade on the wrongs of working women.

"Whether they're teachers or doctors or librarians or clerks at the dry goods counter, women seem to be expected to pay for the privilege of doing anything but housework. It's not fair!"

That was when Harriet made up her mind to tell James that she was unwilling to go on "paying for the privilege" and that he would have to go back to Clatsop, taking Jamie with him. She was still struggling to frame the words that would lift the double burden when a solution presented itself from an unexpected quarter.

The lease on the Clatsop property was for an indefinite period, the tenant having the option to renew yearly, providing that he carried out certain stipulated conditions. The renewal date was approaching and James had asked one of his brothers to make inquiries about the state of the property. He brought the answer he had received for Harriet to read:

"The place is suffering mismanagement and neglect. I spoke with one of your old neighbors last week. He says—among other things—that fences are broken in a number of places. Cattle are straying and not being brought back. As I understand the conditions of your contract, you have grounds for eviction. Would you like me to institute proceedings?"

James was deeply distressed. "I was assured that the Hernstreets would be responsible tenants. Something must have happened to…of course, Cyrus did not inspect the property himself. It's possible that things are not quite as bad as he was told."

"Why don't you go down and see for yourself?" Harriet asked. "Even if everything's as it should be, it won't hurt to remind the tenants of their responsibilities."

James's face brightened—and then clouded. "But what if they're not … if the property is really going to rack and ruin?"

"Then you must turn these tenants out and find better ones. And see to repairing whatever damage has been done."

James started for Clatsop three days later, taking Jamie with him "for company on the trip."

His first letter brought bad news about the fences and good news about Jamie. "He misses you, as I do, but he is himself again now that he is on his beloved farm." The letters that followed were concerned with "the Herculean task" of restoring the buildings and livestock and the "insuperable difficulty" of finding a reliable tenant or manager. As months passed, James had more to say about the former than the latter.

It was nearly midnight when she arrived at the young Carlsons' home, an old frame farmhouse to which had been recently added a two-storey wing divided into two bedrooms and a bath with indoor plumbing.

In one of the upstairs bedrooms the couple's two-year-old son lay dead. He had been sick for only three days. The family doctor who had been treating him had not seemed unduly alarmed and had promised to stop by to check on his condition on the morning of the day that was drawing to a close. Toward noon, the child's breathing had become more and more labored. When the doctor failed to appear, they had tried calling him at his office and his home. There was no answer at either place. The little boy's heart had failed soon after they called Dr. Ferry-Franklin.

All four adults were in a state of barely controlled hysteria. The bereaved and expectant mother was suffering from a dangerous combination of physical and emotional exhaustion. Harriet ordered her to bed and suggested that the elder Mrs. Carlson sit vigil beside her to be sure she rested, even if she could not sleep.

Sally Carlson, the patient to whom she had been called, was bedded down in the parlor. A brief examination of the young woman confirmed Harriet's apprehension: the swollen "bull neck," the fetid odor that issued from the young woman's throat when she obeyed the command to "open as wide as you can," and the frantic gallop of her pulse—all proclaimed diphtheria in a advanced stage, probably too advanced for the antitoxin to do much good. Harriet administered it anyway, asked for a bucket of ice water in which to chill compresses for the swollen neck, and coaxed and bullied the poor girl until she had managed to down a cupful of warm milk, swallow by painful swallow.

"Now lie as still as ever you can, my dear," she said gently. "There was something in the milk for the pain. It'll help you sleep."

When she called the health officer in Yakima, his first question was about the dead child. Had the body been moved? No? Good. It was not to be. And no one was to enter or leave the house until he could get there.

Harriet relayed these orders to the family, gave them directions on the care of the patient, answered their questions as honestly as she could, and started for home.

Dawn was beginning to lighten the sky when she unlocked the door of her office. The window of her waiting room was a dark mirror that reflected a rumpled and bedraggled old woman who had done a night's work few younger women could have done.

She undid the buttons on the pink silk blouse and the hooks at the belt of the skirt, and kicked off the taffeta petticoat and unlaced the flat-front corset, whose stays had been savaging her ribs for hours. (What had possessed her to subject herself to such an instrument of torture?) Too tired to hang her new finery in the armoire, she laid the garments on the bed, into which she longed to climb, put on a more somber and serviceable costume, and went down to make herself a quick breakfast before opening the office to patients.

In the afternoon she made her usual round of house calls and stopped back at the office before returning her horse to the stable. The telephone was ringing. It was Mrs. Carlson, Sr., breathless with panic. Sally had seemed so much better, but now suddenly she was worse. "It's like she's going into a coma."

Harriet said she would come at once.

Mrs. Frobisher's prophecy about a spring storm had finally been fulfilled. Snow was falling so thickly, that Harriet drove the ten miles to the Carlsons' through a blanket of white that blurred the distinction between the road and the ditch beside it, trusting her horse to tell one from the other. Toward the last, he made frequent stops to test the footing before he ventured on. The journey took twice as tong as it should have, but they made it without accident.

The patient was not comatose, but her heart was failing. Harriet injected a stimulant of strychnine. The silent watchers ringing the bedside seemed to be waiting for the poor sufferer to take a breath before they could. She gasped, stirred, sighed—and drew a long, loud breath. Air sucked into the lungs of the watchers and into Harriet's as well.

While she prepared an enema containing a mild stimulant and some nourishment, the senior Carlsons filled her in on what had transpired in the hours she had been absent. The health officer didn't arrive until late in the afternoon. He informed them that in view of the highly infectious character of the disease, he was required by law to remove the body of the child and make arrangements for its burial. The family would be apprised of the location of the grave.

At that point, young Mrs. Carlson all but collapsed, and it looked as if her husband was going to revenge himself on the bearer of these dreadful tidings. But in the end reason had triumphed over anguish.

The health officer disinfected the premises and the family members and told them they were free to come and go as they wished—at least for the present. The elder Mrs. Carlson opted to stay on "so everything wouldn't fall on poor Jenny." Her husband drove the family carriage home to gather up some needed articles and a change of clothing for his wife and to make arrangements for Maia, their youngest daughter, to stay with her married sister until further notice.

"Time I got back here, they said you was on your way," Carlson explained apologetically. "Otherwise I would've gone to fetch you."

The enema acted as Harriet hoped it would. Little by little Sally's breathing eased and she relaxed into sleep. The weary caretakers were sent off to bed and Harriet settled into a chair at the bedside to keep stet until they were rested enough to take over. Watching Sally's face for any sign of a change, she tried to imagine what it had looked like before disease distorted it. Did she resemble her mother, whose features were finely molded although her sallow coloring denied her beauty? Or her father, who reminded Harriet in some way of her own Papa? Sally was her father's favorite as Harriet had been Papa's. How would he have taken it if his "boy" had been snatched from him by death, as this father's child would almost surely be?

She must have dozed a while. When she looked again, the swelling in the girl's face and neck had subsided a little, and the resemblance to her mother was clear. (What a beauty that sad-faced woman must have been in her time.) The fever had also subsided considerably. Harriet fought down a flicker of hope as she felt for a pulse in her patient's wrist. It was rapid and thready—a sign that the heart was inflamed.

Young Leif came in from the kitchen, shaking snow from his coat and cap. He had been out to the barn to see to the stock. He stared down at his sister and asked in a hoarse whisper, "She's some better, ain't she?"

Harriet nodded. "But she requires careful watching. And I must be getting back to town. I have written out the orders you are to follow. Read them carefully and follow them precisely:

"Change the compresses on her neck as often as necessary to be sure that they are cold.

"See to it that she takes fluids every half hour—unless she is asleep—warm milk, water, or clear soup if available.

"Above all, she is not to get out of bed. Someone must be in the room with her at all times to make sure of that.

"Call me if there is any marked change in her condition—either for the better or the worse."

XIII.

The snow had stopped, but there was a bitter wind from the western mountains. By the time she got home, Harriet was stiff cold. She warmed a glass of milk, laced it with brandy, drank it down, and got into bed without bothering to remove the garments she had left on it. She heard the clock strike half past some hour, and then nothing—until a faint, but persistent ringing pulled her toward the surface and its source.

It was the telephone in her office. Groping her way down, she braced herself for news of another crisis in Sally Carlson's illness. But the caller was her friend, Nina Frobisher.

"I'm sorry to disturb you like this, doctor, but I can't sleep for worrying. It's my son's little one—our first grandchild. He wasn't feeling quite himself when we saw him Sunday, so I stopped in this afternoon to make sure he was all right. Before they even opened the door, I could hear the poor little tyke, crying to break your heart! He's running a temperature. His nose is so stopped up he can't breathe through it. And his poor little face is all swollen. They think it's mumps, and they've promised to call you in the morning. But I've been lying here thinking: what if it isn't mumps? What if it's—" She couldn't bring herself to speak the dreaded name. "—what the Carlson baby had? Didn't you say there's a new something you give for it? But if you don't do it early on—" By now she was weeping. "—they don't have much of a chance?"

Harriet spoke a few reassuring words, accepted the offer of the Frobishers' carriage and went upstairs to dress. The clock in office was striking two as she came down. The carriage was waiting at the curb.

Nina's son and his wife were full of apologies for bringing her out at such an hour. "Jackie does have a fever, but he usually does when he's caught cold.

Mother worries too much. If she'd been like this when she was raising us, we'd have had to have a doctor living in the house."

Harriet cut short the apologies and was taken to the nursery where the child lay whimpering in his sleep. He looked to be about the same age as the Carlsons' grandson, but of a sturdier physique. He had all the symptoms of a bad head cold, including a fever, but his face was not as swollen nor his breathing as obstructed as his grandmother had reported. According to his parents, he had swallowed his supper without apparent pain.

Nevertheless, when Harriet was able to persuade him to let her look down his throat, she saw the telltale membrane forming on his tonsils.

The anxious trio watched her rummage in her bag. When she drew out a vial of antitoxin and a syringe, they exchanged a look of alarm.

"Does that mean it is—what Mother was afraid of?"

"It appears to be. But when treatment is started this early, the chances of recovery are excellent—especially in a young, otherwise healthy patient. So it's just as well your mother was worried enough to call me."

"Just as well I knew enough to worry," said Mrs. Frobisher, "which I wouldn't have if you hadn't dressed me down for saying the Carlson girl could wait."

Harriet wrote out detailed instructions for the little patient's care and did what she could—without increasing their anxiety—to impress the family with the importance of following them to the letter. She was back home and in bed by four and slept without dreaming.

She rose at her usual hour of six, took her usual cold shower, ate her usual breakfast, and walked the five blocks to the post office. There was a letter from James which she read as she walked back.

He sounded like his old ebullient self, good-humored, hopeful, enthusiastic—even about the weather, a subject that did not ordinarily engage his attention. Spring was at hand. New grass was pushing up along the dikes. Jamie had seen a whole flock of robins, the fancy kind that looked like they were dressed for a masquerade, and so on and on for a full page.

On the next, as a sort of parenthesis, he mentioned "an extremely flattering offer" which he might be tempted to consider. "A friend of many years has been retained by some eastern businessmen interested in expanding their operation into this quarter of the country. He is charged with recruiting a few citizens of standing who will lend their names and whatever expertise they may possess…in return for which we are to receive a not insubstantial percentage of the profits."

The rest of that page and all of the last one dealt with Franklin family matters. His mother was not well. His sisters-in-law agreed that it would be best for her to sell the house and move in with one or the other of them. James was included in the family council that was attempting to decide which, or whether the burden—and the honor—should be shared.

"And by the by, it is astonishing and deeply gratifying to how their attitude toward you has changed. I believe they are ready to recognize you for the angel I know you to be. Some generous gesture on your part would go far toward hastening that happy end."

The letter was signed, "Your affectionate husband."

The sun was bright, but not warm enough to melt the snow on the roads, so she had her horse hitched to a sleigh for the drive out to the Carlsons.

Phrases from James's letter kept echoing in her head—little bursts of words that kept time to the rhythm of the hoof beats and stirred suspicions that creaked like the joints of the sleigh. Who was the "friend of many years?" Who were the "we" whose names and expertise were to be rewarded? Apparently, James was one, but who were the others? One or both of his ne'er-do-well brothers? What "friend of many years" could be ignorant of their record of financial fecklessness? And what sort of eastern business—except a railroad—would have any interest in this far corner of the continent?

James's other news was also unsettling. That he had made peace with his family was to have been expected. But what had wrought this miraculous change in their attitude toward her? And what generous gesture would be required to guarantee its permanence?

Her mind leaped to the connection: railroads. They were an addiction of James's. A speculator who wanted to ensnare him had only to mention the word. That must be what had happened. The mysterious friend was another fly-by-night promoter who knew James's reputation as an easy gull. He had got to James through his brothers, neither of whom had anything to contribute—or to lose. What James had was land—the land she was fighting so desperately to save. The generous gesture would turn out to be permission to encumber the property to raise capital for another doomed venture.

Nothing in this world would persuade her to grant such permission, but what if James were prevailed upon, or tricked into pledging it without asking. He had done that once before. How, short of standing constant guard over him, could she prevent him?

The sleigh turned up the lane that led to the Carlsons' yard, and she turned—almost with relief—to the consideration of problems with which she was competent to deal.

Her patient was better than she had any reason to hope. Sally had had the first good night's sleep since her illness began, and the improvement was so striking that Harriet had to caution the family not to assume that the danger was over. For the moment, it was young Jenny Carlson whose condition concerned her. She was in last two months of her pregnancy and in an alarming state of exhaustion.

Her husband reported that she had insisted on sitting vigil beside Sally all through the night. "It seems like she's blaming herself. If Sal hadn't come out to give us a hand, she wouldn't have come down sick. They're real fond of each other, Jen and Sal. Went to school together and been friends ever since."

Harriet spoke sternly to the culprit. "Wearing yourself out worrying will not help to pull her through. Your obligation is to the baby you are carrying. I want you off your feet for the rest of the day and in bed for the whole of the night." And to Mrs. Carlson, Sr., "You need rest almost as much as she does. Aren't there some neighbor women you can get to come in and help?"

Mrs. Carlson looked to her son for an answer. He shook his head.

"There hasn't anyone been by since it got out what the sickness is. Everybody's afraid it's catching."

With which Harriet could not argue.

The anxiety she had suppressed during her visit returned, intensified, on the journey back to town. Recognizing the enemy did not arm her against him—or them. One way to thwart the schemers was to alert the holders of the mortgages. But she had been warned that they could at any time and for any reason demand immediate payment in full. On the other hand, it was she, not James, they had been persuaded to trust. If there was some way to assure them that she was not a party to whatever folly James was about to commit.

Sometimes one saw notices in the newspapers in which husbands announced to whomever it concerned that they would no longer be responsible for debts incurred by their wives. She could not recall having seen such a declaration made by a wife, but that might not mean it was impossible.

One thing was certain: she needed advice from someone knowledgeable in matters of business and law. But from whom could she ask it? Isaac and

Ellen were on a buying trip to New York. Rob had moved away. She could write him, but it would be Nora who answered. (The conviction had been growing in her mind of late that the antagonism between his wife and his mother was one of the factors in Rob's decision to move his practice for the second time.)

The only lawyer she had retained was the one who obtained her divorce from Will Ross, and he must be dead long since. The terms of that divorce included a provision that released her from responsibility for Will's debts.

She had grounds for divorcing James, more valid than those that won her freedom from Will—at least to those Christians who held that infidelity alone justified dissolving the marriage tie. But she had not pressed that claim when it was new. To do so now would do irreparable injury to the child who still considered her his mother. It would also expose the perjury she and James had committed when they went through the legal adoption proceedings and swore that Jamie had no living parent.

And after all, it was not James's infidelity that was driving her to despair. It was the almost intolerable burden he had become.

She reached home just before noon, and found Mr. Carlson, Sr., waiting with a team to drive her to his own house, eleven miles to the east. He had heard the good news about Sally, but now his youngest daughter was giving him cause for concern.

"Maia's got a sore throat and a terrible bad headache." He wanted to be sure it wasn't "something she caught at Leif's when she was helping them out" and to have the doctor take measures to stave it off if it was.

Maia Carlson was still in her teens, built solidly like her father, and in generally good health. She showed several of the early symptoms of diphtheria, but—as in the case of the Frobisher baby—Harriet felt confident that the antitoxin would do its work before the disease progressed to its virulent stage.

She gave the injection and wrote out the same list of strict instructions for nursing care. As she wrote "complete bed rest," it struck her that she needed rest almost as much as her patient did. Two hours of sleep in the last—was it two days or three? In any case, it was not enough. She must steal at least an hour from her afternoon's schedule for a nap.

But before she had finished her instructions, the telephone rang. Leif Carlson was calling to say that Sally seemed to be having a bad spell. Could the doctor come back?

How could she refuse? Perhaps she could sleep a little while Carlson drove. But he could not leave Maia. She had just written "not under any circumstances is she to be left unattended."

"Is there someone who can stay with Maia for as long as it takes you to drive me home?" she asked. "I can drive my own carriage from there."

"Well, there's Britta. She could, I expect. But we'd have to drive over there to ask. They don't have a phone."

"Does she have a neighbor who does and could get a message to her?"

Carlson looked dubious. "We could drive by there on our way—except it ain't really on the way. And then she might not be home. Wait now! Didn't she say something about meaning to take the baby to see his other grandmother? That'd be in town."

The logistics had become too complicated for Harriet to sort out. The only solution she could think of was to borrow Carlsons' carriage and drive herself, but she was not sure she was up to the challenge of managing a strange team. Fortunately, Carlson remembered that one of his neighbors (who did have a telephone) sometimes hired out his team.

"He can drive you out in my rig. That way I've still got my team and the wagon, if it's needed."

Harriet climbed into the carriage, wrapped herself up against the cold, closed her eyes, and summoned sleep. It neither obeyed nor defied the summons. She wandered in a limbo between waking and dreaming, reliving strangely altered versions of the events of the last two days, in which both the players and their afflictions kept changing. Always just when she was on the point of administering some remedy, she was called away or otherwise interfered with. Once when she was ready to give an injection, she discovered that the vials of antitoxin she had brought along were all empty.

That brought her awake, but when she dozed again, disasters threatened. Small problems she could have foreseen and forestalled if she had not been so beset turned into life-threatening blunders. The harder she strove to put them right, the more she erred.

The end of the journey put an end to the nightmare, but left her no more rested than she had been at the start.

Sally Carlson was dying. Harriet heard it in her breathing and saw it in her face. Her own face relayed the verdict to the three who stood just inside the parlor door. Jenny groaned, clutched her distended belly, and cried out that her pains had started. Mrs. Carlson had dropped her head into her hands and was weeping hysterically. Leif looked from his sister to his wife to his mother and seemed to freeze. Harriet took Mrs. Carlson by the shoulders and forced her into a chair. To Leif she said crisply, "Carry your wife upstairs. Put her to bed and keep her there, while I prepare an injection."

"One like you gave Sal? That means she's—"

"She's going into labor well ahead of her time. What I give her may slow it a little."

Leif did as he was ordered. Harriet mixed a sedative for the elder Mrs. Carlson and filled a syringe with a powerful opiate for Jenny. By the time both had been administered, the house was quiet. She pulled a chair to the dying girl's bedside and reached for her hand.

It gripped hers so tightly that Harriet's arthritic fingers complained. Little by little, as the pain lessened, Sally's hand relaxed, but it did not let go.

Time passed slowly. Sally's breathing was light and shallow, but steady. Harriet's picked up the same cadence. It seemed to her that they were merging into a single being, swimming in the same dark current toward the same unknown, unknowable end.

She slept.

When she woke, their hands were still joined, but Sally was no longer breathing. Nothing was changed, but nothing was the same.

They had traveled a long way together—two strangers—moving with the dark current toward light. But the light faded, and Harriet was alone. The darkness wrapped arms of silence around her and healed her.

She disengaged her hand, laid Sally's on her breast and went upstairs to the bedroom where Leif kept watch over his mother and his wife. Both were sleeping soundly. Jenny's pains had stopped—at least for the present. Harriet did not need words to convey her news. Leif sighed and bowed his head. The silence embraced them all.

She called the health officer to report the death and the threat of premature birth. "The sooner you can get here, the better. For, as you know as well as anyone, if a child is born into this infected house, it's unlikely that either it or the mother will survive."

He had been on the point of retiring for the evening, and it took a good deal of persuading to convince him that the situation was as critical as Harriet considered it. Finally it was agreed that if Harriet would call the undertaker and give him measurements for a coffin, both men would start as soon as "the necessary preparations" could be completed.

But that would be several hours, and Harriet decided to spend them in the chair beside Sally's bed, sleeping if she could or, if not, trying to think her way through the tangle of problems she had brought with her to this house of death.

The silence still filled her head and heart, drowning out the discords that had distracted and deafened her.

She stood on a high place, breathing air too thin to sustain the emotions—anger and fear, desire and guilt—that had warred within her, looking down on the landscape of her life. From this perspective all the hills and valleys, rough places and smooth, were merged into a geography of meaning.

Some of the patterns were familiar and comforting; others were disturbing revelations. She had not realized till how very much alone she was. Friends she still had, many of long years standingbut no intimates. Some she had lost to death—Papa, Sis, Lyman, and just this past year, Mama. Others had drifted too far away to be reclaimed. Some—like Will—she had turned against in anger; some had turned against her—Jamie for one. Some she had lost by asking more of them than they were able to give. To others she had given too little, or not given what was asked at the time it was wanted. It was her fault in some cases, not in others. The prospect of a lonely old age was not to be altered by assigning blame. But it was at least mitigated by one consoling exception.

Ellen—dear, generous Ellen—who had asked nothing and given whatever she had to give, who had forgiven her sister's sins, both of commission and omission, except perhaps for one—Harriet's rejection of Aaron.

That was the most painful of revelations. Even now she could not have borne the shame of it without the strength she drew from the silence she still carried within her.

❧

She had not simply rejected Aaron. She had reneged on a promise. Not a promise spoken, but a promise nonetheless. When she set off for Philadelphia, it was understood between them that when she came back, Aaron would propose again and she would accept. But when that day came, her feelings had changed. Or, with the honesty her new perspective forced, not so much her feelings, as her values. They had been altered by the opinion of people she despised.

In Philadelphia, she encountered, not among the Friends with whom she studied, but in some other groups with which she mingled, a prejudice against Jews. Something so new to her that it took some time to accept its existence. Back in Roseburg, Isaac Rose and Aaron Weiss were considered leading citizens and public benefactors. The Ferry family's fortunes were on the decline and Ellen's marriage to a prosperous merchant was considered a coup. Harriet's marriage to his partner would have assured her as secure a place in the local society as Ellen enjoyed. The bigots of Philadelphia would have been forgotten. But before she was settled into her new profession—before Aaron had chosen a propitious moment to press his suit—the scandal over the autopsy drove her into exile. In Portland, she found herself associating with people—met through her practice—whose disdain for "those of the Hebrew persuasion" was flagrant. It shocked and angered her, but not enough to move her to speak out in dissent.

When Ellen and Isaac established themselves in Portland, she saw her sister snubbed in ways that made her cheeks burn, but which Ellen seemed determined not to notice. They had never discussed this. Why? In those days they had confided to each other more often and more freely than at any other time of their lives. But on this important topic, not a whisper. Harriet wondered sometimes whether Ellen assumed that her sister shared her view that such snobbery was beneath their notice. Or was Ellen as reluctant as she to face what such a discussion would reveal?

Aaron was too sensitive not to have sensed the change. When he wound up the business in Roseburg and came to join Isaac, he and Harriet saw each other often. At first she was uneasy in his presence. But as time passed and he never renewed his offer, she took comfort in the belief that it was his feelings, not hers, that had cooled.

Ellen had always assumed a connection between her rejection of Aaron and her acceptance of James, which Harriet had always denied. But there was a connection—not a simple matter of choosing one over the other—but a common cause: the obsession that had fastened itself upon her long, long ago: she struggled to live down one disgrace after another, to be accepted, respectable—a member of the elite.

She, who had thought herself a rebel, defying custom and convention. A pathfinder, like Miss Anthony and Mrs. Duniway, who had spent her girlhood railing against being cabined, cribbed, and confined by the accident of sex. She, who had bloodied her head more than once trying to break through the walls of that prison, had turned cowardly when faced with a critical choice. Had bowed to the dictates of a public opinion that penalized women for exceeding its expectations of them. The rebel had stooped to reenter the prison and pulled the door shut behind her.

Now, on the verge of old age, she was faced with another such choice. But if her courage failed her again, she knew where to look for strength.

It was past midnight when the health officer and the undertaker arrived. An hour later, they had done their work and were ready to start back. There was room in their carriage for the doctor if she wanted to be dropped off at home. She thanked them, but said she was still needed here.

She spent the rest of the night disinfecting the sickroom, carrying out the infected bedding and burying it in the snow, and making preparations for the premature birth, if it came. (Jenny's pains had not recurred and Harriet was beginning to hope that the omen had been averted.) Mrs. Carlson was awake and anxious to be given "something, anything," to do. The health officer had left a large bottle of disinfectant. Harriet showed her how to use it and set her to work on the kitchen, the rail of the stairway, and door knobs all over the house.

Leif came to ask if they ought to call his father. His mother said no. Let him sleep if he could, time enough to burden him in the morning.

It was still dark when Harriet heard Mr. Carlson's carriage in the lane. She threw a shawl over her shoulders and went out to greet him with news she was not sure he could bear to hear.

When he understood that his favorite child was dead and already buried, he went so white that she thought he was going to faint. But after a moment, he said, simply, "We must still care for the living."

He had come on behalf of his oldest daughter. Britta had come to give him a hand with Maia. She had brought her boy with her. Now both were complaining of sore throats. Britta had done some of the nursing of her sister and nephew, so it was likely she had caught the plague at the same source. Shouldn't they be given the injection that would avert the illness?

Harriet and Mrs. Carlson went upstairs to check on Jenny's condition. She was awake and restless, but the pains had not recurred.

"You go on, doctor," Mrs. Carlson said. "I can look after her now."

"The pains may start again."

"I been a midwife enough times to know what to do if they do. If there's complications, we can call you. There's nothing going to happen so fast you can't get back."

Back at the senior Carlsons' Harriet found the oldest daughter watching at her sister's bedside and trying to quiet her fretful child lest he wake the sleeper. Neither she nor the baby had as yet symptoms that would have warranted a prophylactic injection under normal circumstances, but an epidemic was not normal circumstances. She injected mother and child and instructed Britta to keep the baby as inactive as possible and be careful not to overtire herself.

She was giving instructions on procedures to minimize the danger of infection—how to disinfect clothing and bedding and dishes—when she noticed that Maia had waked and was listening with interest.

"Is there something you want, my dear?" she asked.

Maia smiled wanly, shook her head, and then blurted in a rusty croak, "I want to be a doctor."

"Do you now? And when did you decide that?" Harriet spoke in the patronizing tone adults use on children who are not to be taken seriously.

"Ever since she was knee high to a grasshopper," Britta answered for her sister, and went on to tell how, as a child, Maia had spent hours medicating and bandaging her dolls. "Nowadays, it's Billy. I don't like to leave him with her anymore for fear she'll start doctoring on him."

Harriet felt the girl's forehead. The fever had abated, but not broken yet. Her pulse was almost normal. She was definitely on the mend.

"If you want to be a doctor," she said sententiously, "you must learn that your first responsibility is to your own health." (A maxim she was not observing at the moment.) "I want you to stay in bed, drink as much liquid as possible, talk no more than is absolutely necessary, and sleep. That is the medicine you need now."

Maia nodded gravely. "I'm going to get better," she said. It was a declarative sentence, but there was the hint of a question in the end.

"Yes, indeed you are," Harriet said. "If you follow all those rules."

Obediently, Maia closed her eyes.

Carlson left her at her own door. Harriet muffled the telephone in her office and went straight up to bed, determined to get enough sleep to sustain her through the winding down of this ordeal, and the ordeals that would flow from the decisions she had made sometime in the long night of watching.

She was going to divorce James Franklin. Not because he had been unfaithful or improvident. Not to save the property she had intended to depend on when she was no longer able to work. Not for any of the reasons that might have moved her before the silence showed her the landscape of her life. The pattern that gave meaning to the whole was the work itself. She would be doing that work, if not for as long as she lived, at least as far into the future as she could see. Not doing all she could have if she had started sooner and the slope had not been so slippery. There was still much she needed to learn, but it was not too late to being the learning.

That was why she was going to cut the tie to James and his son, because she could not carry the burden they had become and get on with her work.

Divorce, or separation, or whatever sort of arrangement would set her free, would cost something. Not only money, but the good opinion of many people, some she loved, and some for whom she felt little or nothing. It was possible that she would not be invited to join the Ladies Reading Club after all. But the future she was planning would leave little time for the pleasures of such society. Nora's disapproval might finalize her estrangement from Rob, and as a corollary, from Rogie, and leave her even more alone than she was now.

But she would be climbing the right slope at last. And there might be other companions as yet unknown, other, younger women who had heard the same call.

Maia Carlson was about the age her own lost daughter would have been. There was no one to do for Maia what Harriet had planned to do for her own little girl. If Maia was really called to the profession…or if not she, then some other young woman – or women! There must be many of them. She would make them all her daughters, stretch out her hand to as many as she could reach, and start them on their climb. The slope would not be as steep or as slippery as it had been for her, but there would still be pitfalls. She would point them out, show them how to keep their footing when some male boot sent the sand sliding down, teach them the lessons it had cost her so much to learn.

Or did each generation have to learn these lessons for itself? ✺

Afterword:
Dr. Bethenia Owens-Adair

By Cathy Croghan Alzner

The Slope is a fictional rendering of a period in the life of one of Oregon's most remarkable women, Dr. Bethenia Owens-Adair.

Dr. Bethenia Owens-Adair was an Oregon Trail emigrant, arguably the state's first woman medical doctor, and a tireless reformer. She made notable contributions to several social movements, including temperance, women's suffrage, the preservation of Oregon pioneer history, and women's advancement in the medical profession; she walked "the various avenues of industry" to "earn her honest bread by the side of her brother, man." She spent a lifetime combating prejudices and overcoming societal and economic hurdles. In a time of few rights for women, she challenged divorce and child custody laws. At the same time, Owens-Adair experienced an often-difficult personal life that she struggled to balance with the demands of a rigorous profession.

Bethenia Owens was born on February 2, 1840, in Van Buren County, Missouri, to Sarah and Thomas Owens, the third of their eleven children. In 1843, when she was three years old, the family joined that year's group of emigrants to the Oregon Country, first settling near the mouth of the Columbia River south of present-day Astoria. Here they farmed wheat, flax, and cranberries, and raised dairy cattle. Few opportunities, including education, existed then for girls. Bethenia felt constrained by the female gender role norms and regretted that she had not been born a boy. In A Souvenir: Dr. Owens-Adair to Her Friends, she stated, "I realized that a girl was hampered and hemmed in on all sides simply by accident of sex."

Independent by nature, from an early age Bethenia was also compassionate and caring, tending her numerous younger siblings. The family moved to the Umpqua Valley in 1852, and there, on her fourteenth birthday, May 4, 1854, Bethenia married Legrand H. Hill, with whom she soon had a son, George.

Hill was abusive to both Bethenia and George. In 1859, at age nineteen, she sued for and won a divorce by an act of the Oregon Territorial Governor, as well as custody of George and the return of her maiden name. By 1867, she was established in a millinery shop in Clatsop County. Her business prospered and she was able to send George to University of California at Berkeley, still longing for the education she had been denied.

Owens had long been interested in medicine, so in 1871 she bought a copy of Grey's Anatomy and began planning how she could attend medical school. In 1873, at the age of thirty-three, Owens boarded a train for Philadelphia, where she entered the Eclectic School of Medicine. Owens completed her course of study and graduated in the following year, when she returned to Oregon and established a practice in Portland. Industrious and competent, Dr. Owens prospered. She was able to pay all expenses for George to attend the Willamette University School of Medicine in Salem, and her generosity extended to others in need; she financed the college education of a sister, and supported and educated the daughter of one of her patients.

Unsatisfied with the quality of her medical training, Bethenia determined to become a full-fledged doctor of medicine, despite the open hostility of most medical schools to female students. Her efforts paid off when she was accepted at the University of Michigan in 1878, and received her degree at Ann Arbor in 1880. Again she returned to Portland, now a credentialed medical doctor.

In 1884, Owens-Adair's life changed dramatically. Though she had been single for twenty-five years, she then married Col. John Adair of Astoria, a West Point graduate and a longtime friend. In her mid-forties, a surprised Bethenia discovered that she was pregnant. The infant girl, born in 1887, lived but a few days, and her death left Owens-Adair distraught and grief-stricken. She closed her Portland practice, and moved to a farm near Astoria with her family. In 1891, the Adairs adopted a grandson whose mother had died; they also adopted a newborn girl who was the daughter of one of Bethenia's patients who also had died.

John Adair was involved in land and railroad speculation in the area; the railroad line ran within view of their farm, Sunnymead. However, it was Bethenia's medical practice that kept the family afloat financially. Despite severe rheumatism that caused her to close her office and remain on the farm, she could not quit doctoring. It was not unusual for her to respond to a call in the middle of the night during a torrential Oregon downpour. In the midst of these changes, her husband recklessly pursued schemes that edged them toward financial ruin. They divorced in 1907.

Bethenia Owens-Adair's life experiences propelled her into active participation in several reform movements, including those for temperance, woman suffrage, and eugenics. Eugenics, based on the belief that some "maladies" could be "cured" by preventing the individual from reproducing and thus passing along their undesirable traits, was based on an interpretation of Darwinian science that is no longer in repute and that many persons today view as repugnant. It is important to realize that in advocating human sterilization in particular instances, Owens-Adair and her colleagues were motivated by compassion. Although Owens-Adair was criticized for her efforts, she persevered, believing she was helping to save people from a miserable existence and helping to improve the happiness and safety of future generations. The state eugenics board was finally established in 1923; it was abolished in 1983.

Bethenia Owens-Adair dedicated her life to helping others. She fought gender constrictions to secure to herself and others the rights that society had long denied to women. She was a strong voice for temperance and for human sterilization, motivated by a desire to reduce human suffering. She worked tirelessly for causes she believed would be beneficial to the citizens of Oregon. Bethenia Owens-Adair died at Sunnymead on September 11, 1926.

Cathy Croghan Alzner is an instructor in history at Portland Community College, where she teaches courses on United States history, American women, and the American West. She holds degrees from Pacific Lutheran University and Portland State University.

Cast of characters

The Slope is a work of fiction. The characters, however, are based upon real persons. This partial list of characters is paired with the name of the historical personage that she or he represents, for the benefit of readers with a historical perspective.

The Slope	Historical personage
Harriet Franklin	Bethenia Owens-Adair
William Ross	Legrand Hill
Robert Ross	George Hill (son)
Roger Ross	Victor Hill (grandson)
James Franklin	John Adair
Jamie Franklin	John Adair, Jr. (adopted son)
Col. and Mrs. Franklin	Col. and Mrs. John Adair (John's parents)
Cyrus Franklin	William Adair (John's brother)
Isaac Rose	Hyman Abraham
Mama Ferry	Sarah Damron Owens
Papa Ferry	Thomas Owens

Acknowledgements

I found Bethenia in the Astoriana Collection in the Astor Library in Astoria, Oregon, and received help in further research from its librarian, Bruce Berney, his assistant, Jerre Engeman, and Children's Librarian Juanita Price. Jerre lived in a house once occupied by Bethenia and helped me go through its attic closets looking for correspondence (which we didn't find). Juanita gave me a snapshot she had taken of the little house Bethenia had built in Astoria when she lived there and worked as a milliner

Gravestones in Warrenton's Ocean View Cemetery separated Bethenia and her baby daughter from the Adair family, and I was still puzzling over the reason when Bruce Berney showed me a University of Oregon graduate thesis by Carol McFarland that had just been presented to the Astoriana Collection. It solved the mystery and threw light on the rest of Bethenia's long, sometimes lonely autumn years.

The Reverend Sallie Shippen let me read some letters of Bethenia's in the archives of Astoria's Grace Episcopal Church, and I was able to search in the vaults of the Clatsop County Courthouse for financial records that explained why she was buried—when I first saw it—in what amounted to a pauper's grave.

I also read in the Oregon Historical Society's collection the correspondence between Bethenia and Jesse Applegate, "the Sage of Yoncalla," who had carried Bethenia on his shoulders when her family emigrated from Missouri.

And finally it was the devotion of friends of mine and of Bethenia's who made it possible to overcome a formidable array of obstacles and contretemps and bring this book to print. Chief among them are Bette Sinclair, Diane Heintz, and Richard Engeman. I am deeply grateful to all of them.